My Biggest Bedtime Storybook

Brimax Books · Newmarket · England

Contents

Sammy Scarecrow's Party

For year after year Sammy Scarecrow had stood in Farmer Green's field forgotten. His clothes had become old and tattered, and his hat was full of holes. Then one evening, the Wood Wizard stepped out of the wood and said: "Sammy, tomorrow is your twenty-first birthday, and the woodland folk have decided to give a party for you. The birds and the bees have promised to take the invitations out. The party will begin at sunset, so stay awake, Sammy."

Sammy had never been so excited. He didn't know what to do with himself all next day. At sunset the Wood Wizard stepped out of the wood again. He handed Sammy a little box. "Many happy returns of your twenty-first birthday, Sammy."

Eagerly Sammy opened the box. Inside was a tiny acorn, and underneath it was written:-

Plant me in a moonbeam's glow;
Water me to make me grow.

Before the moon rose, the guests began to arrive. The Elfin Folk flew in on the backs of moths. Leprechauns galloped in on Irish jaunting carts. They wore green suits with feathers in their hats. The Fairy Queen came in grand style in a coach drawn by a long team of ants, with ladybirds as footmen. Dwarfs rode in on the backs of moles from underground tunnels.

Kelpies arrived on tiny horses, and a party of gnomes marched in singing and playing musical instruments.

All the guests brought presents. Sammy was thrilled when he found among them a new red overcoat for the winter, a pair of baggy blue trousers, a yellow scarf, and a shiny top hat for his head. "Thank you, thank you!" he cried, "I do wish I had a feast for our guests."

"It's time you planted your acorn," the Wood Wizard said. "Look! The moon has risen."

Carefully Sammy planted the acorn in the path of a moonbeam, and watered it. In moments it became a great oak-tree.

Sammy cried out in delight. The Wood Wizard, wearing his tall pointed hat, stepped to the tree, stretched out his hand towards it, and called out in a loud voice:-

"Birthday tree, to be of use
Show the guests what you produce."

At once things began to appear on the tree, on twigs and branches and leaves—fudge, candies, liquorice, jellies of different colours, ice-creams, dewdrop drinks, cakes, cookies, tasty titbits of all kinds.

Sammy cried out delightedly: "Please help yourselves!" The guests did help themselves; but whatever they took from the tree was at once replaced by another ice-cream or cake or whatever it was. The Wood Wizard cried:-

Now feast all night and dance with glee
Round Sammy Scarecrow's birthday tree!"

12

Dance and feast the guests did, until at last the Wood Wizard held up his hand and cried:-

"Midnight is about to strike.
Candles, candles, come alight!"

There was a flash, and twenty-one candles lit up on the tree. Everyone cheered and clapped. Linking hands, all the guests danced round the tree, singing "Happy birthday to you, happy birthday to you, happy birthday, dear Sammy, happy birthday to you!"

They danced and sang and feasted until somewhere a clock struck twelve—midnight. The candles went out. The tree shrank into the ground. The guests whispered goodnight to Sammy and stole away. Soon all was silent.

"Thank you, Wood Wizard!" cried Sammy. "Thank you, all! I'll never, never forget this wonderful party."

Well, if ever you see a scarecrow in a field wearing a red overcoat, baggy blue trousers, a yellow scarf, and a top hat set at a jaunty angle on his head, you'll know it's Sammy Scarecrow, and *you* will remember his wonderful twenty-first birthday party, won't you?

The Golden Goose

Once there was a man who had three sons. One day the eldest went to the forest to chop wood. At midday, as he was eating his lunch, an old man appeared from nowhere and asked for a small bite to eat.

"Go away," said the eldest son, "I share my lunch with no one."

He didn't know the old man had magic powers, and he thought it was just bad luck when his axe slipped as he worked that afternoon, and he cut his thumb.

The following day the middle
son went to the forest. At midday the
old man appeared again. The
middle son was as greedy and as
ill mannered as his elder
brother.

"Go away," he said, "I share
my lunch with no one." He too
thought it was just bad luck when
a log fell on his toe and bruised it
so badly that he limped all the
way home.

On the third day it was the turn
of the third and youngest son to
go to the forest to chop wood.

At midday, as the youngest son,
who was called Dummling, sat
eating his lunch the old man
appeared yet again, and once
more asked for a small bite to
eat.

"Come and sit beside me," said
Dummling. "What is mine is
yours also. Eat your fill."

When the old man had finished
every scrap of Dummling's lunch
he pointed to an old and rotting
tree stump.

"Cut that down," he said, "and
you will find a reward for having
a kind heart." And with that, he
disappeared as mysteriously as
he had arrived.

Dummling was curious, and thought the tree was too old and rotten to be of any use to a wood-cutter, he chopped it down as the old man had suggested. Lying unharmed at the base of the stump, on a bed of dried leaves, was a goose with golden feathers. It let Dummling stroke its head, and nestled quietly in his arms when he picked it up.

"I can't leave you here," said Dummling. "Someone is sure to kill you for the sake of your golden feathers. I think I had better take you with me."

Dummling was a long way from home and he decided to spend the night at an inn. The landlord of the inn had three daughters. One of them looked enviously at the goose's golden feathers and made up her mind to have one.

That night as Dummling lay asleep, she tried to pluck a feather from the goose's back. She touched the goose very gently, she didn't want it to make a noise and wake Dummling, but as she grasped the feather and tried to pull it she found to her dismay that her hand would not move.

She tried to let go of the feather and found that she couldn't. "Oh . . . oh . . ." she cried softly, "My hand is stuck fast . . . Sister, please pull me away."

Her sister came to help her, but as soon as she touched her dress she found that she was stuck too. The same thing happened to the third sister when she tried to pull the second sister free.

Dummling had decided to see something of the world before he went home, and the next day he set off across country with the golden goose tucked safely under his arm. He did not seem to notice the three sisters trailing awkwardly behind him like a broken daisy chain. He didn't seem to notice either when a disapproving clergyman tried to pull the girls away and was caught himself. Or the clergyman's young assistant who could not let go of the clergyman's coat tails. Or for that matter the three diggers who were going home to lunch when they joined in the game, and discovered too late that it wasn't a game at all. Or, if Dummling did notice, he pretended not to.

He had heard of a King whose daughter had been promised in marriage to anyone who could make her smile.

When the sad Princess saw Dummling with his golden goose tucked under his arm and all the people tagging along behind, the first one stuck to the goose and the rest stuck to one another as if by magic (which they were of course), and all tripping over one another's heels and bumping into one another's elbows, she not only smiled, she laughed until she cried, as did everyone else who saw that strange procession.

Dummling and the Princess were married, and lived happily ever after. No one knows what happened to the golden goose and the people who were stuck to it. Maybe the magic wore off. Maybe it didn't. Maybe they are wandering still.

THE DRAGON OF DUMBY

The citizens of Dumby were worried. Every week one of their enemies attacked them.

"What we need is a dragon," said the Mayor. "A big, fierce dragon."

"We did have one, a long time ago," mumbled old Mr Snoddy. "But he grew old and useless, like me. We never replaced him. Expensive monsters, dragons."

"We could get one from the Wildlife Dragon Park," said the Mayor. So he sent a telegram. Early next morning, he had a reply. It read:

GOOD QUALITY DRAGON ARRIVING AT TEN O'CLOCK. DO NOT OVERFEED HIM. CAN BE EXCHANGED IF UNSATISFACTORY.

As the city clock chimed ten, a long, narrow cart rattled into the cobbled square. Inside was a long, narrow dragon.

The mayor stepped forward to make a speech of welcome, as the dragon clambered out of the cart, wagging his tail. The Mayor was taken aback. "You should look much fiercer than that!" he exclaimed.

The dragon looked surprised. "I'm not fierce at all!" he said, in a jolly voice.

The children were delighted with the dragon. They crowded round, touching his scaly green skin.

"You're not as big as we expected," said Pip, the baker's son.

The dragon looked wistful. "I'd like to be bigger," he said, "but dragons come in different sizes, just like people."

"What's your name?" asked one of the children.

The dragon looked bashful. "Promise you won't laugh," he said. Everyone promised. "It's Dermot," he went on, "but I'd rather be called Fred."

"Nonsense!" said the Mayor briskly. "Fred's no name for a dragon—it wouldn't frighten a fly! Dermot you're called, and Dermot you'll stay."

He looked the dragon over. "What do you eat?" he asked.

Dermot licked his lips. "Cucumber," he said. "Celery, and rhubarb."

The Mayor groaned. "All long, thin food!" he said. "No wonder you're *that* shape."

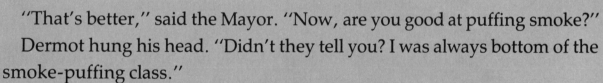

So Dermot was put on a 'round' diet; melons, pumpkins, dumplings, and Christmas puddings. One day he even swallowed Pip's football by mistake. He doubled his size in less than a week.

"That's better," said the Mayor. "Now, are you good at puffing smoke?"

Dermot hung his head. "Didn't they tell you? I was always bottom of the smoke-puffing class."

The Mayor was worried. What was the use of a dragon who couldn't puff? He began to think seriously of asking for an exchange dragon.

Early next morning, Billy the Bugler, who'd been on night patrol, sounded the alert.

Dermot, who slept in a railway tunnel because it was the same shape as himself, woke with a start. The Mayor snatched off his nightcap and jumped out of bed. "It's the Bandidados—they always attack on Tuesdays!" he cried.

Captain Beat-e-moff was giving orders to Dumby's small army. "Push out the cannon!" he shouted.

The cannon creaked, squeaked, and wobbled.

"Can't you oil it?" said the Mayor irritably.

"Sorry," said the Captain. "But the King wanted the oil for his armour."

His Majesty tottered out of the Palace, calling in a quavery voice: "Where's my good old Dando?"

Dando was brought from his stable, wearing his shabby old saddle.

"Don't forget his glasses!" said the King. "He can't see the enemy without them!"

It took five soldiers to heave His Majesty onto Dando's back.

"Where's the new dragon?" quavered the King. "He must come in front with me."

Dermot groaned. Fighting was such a silly waste of time, but he would have to do his best. The people of Dumby had given him a home—he must try and repay them.

The procession moved out of the city gate. The King wobbled so much that his armour rattled. The enemy came in sight. A hundred fierce Bandidados, wearing their red helmets with green feathers at the side. In front was the biggest, fiercest dragon Dermot had ever seen. Smoke poured from his nostrils, and he was roaring in fine style.

The King looked down at Dermot. "We haven't got a chance against this lot, have we, dragon?" he quavered.

Dermot shook his head in despair. Then he took a deep breath. Making a great effort, he managed to puff a very small cloud of smoke.

"I did it!" he shouted. He went on puffing. The clouds got bigger.

Captain Beat-e-moff was delighted. "Dragon – forward – CHARGE!" he yelled.

Dermot rushed forward. Soon the Bandidados and their dragon were struggling in a thick fog of smoke. Then Captain Beat-e-moff sent Billy the Bugler round behind the enemy. When he sounded the attack, the Bandidados thought the Dumby army was behind them. They turned and rushed off down the hill.

Dermot was a hero.

"I knew you could do it if you tried!" beamed the Mayor, crossing Tuesday off the calendar. "Now just keep in practice for Thursday, young Dermot. That's when we expect the Black Baron and his Boldos. They're a *very* nasty crowd."

But early next morning there was a shout from Captain Beat-e-moff. "Enemy in sight!" he yelled.

"It's not even Thursday!" gasped the Mayor.

Dermot's heart sank. He hoped his puff was in good order.

"Never mind about the King," shouted the Captain. "There's no time to get him mounted. Come along, young dragon-me-lad!"

The Boldos, looking very villainous, were already half way across Dumby Marsh. In front was an enormous, roaring dragon.

Poor Dermot was terrified. *His* smoke would be little use against such a monster. How he wished he was back at the Wildlife Park!

Then an amazing thing happened. The enemy dragon stopped, and stared. "Dermot!" he roared, a broad grin spreading across his huge scaly face.

"Cyril!" squeaked Dermot, running forward.

The two armies were so surprised that they sat down to watch.

"When did you leave the Wildlife Park?" asked Cyril.

Dermot told him everything.

"I'm at Morrogan," said Cyril. "They're not a bad lot, but they will keep fighting! I put on a show to please them, but I do wish they'd give it up."

"So do I!" Dermot was delighted that Cyril felt the same.

"Why don't we start a Peaceful Dragon Club?" said Cyril.

So they did. In less than a week every dragon for miles around had joined. So there was no more fighting.

The citizens of Dumby were delighted, and very proud of Dermot.

As Pip said: "He may *look* big and fierce, but inside he's the gentlest dragon in the world!"

So the Mayor sent a telegram to the Wildlife Park. It read: "Completely satisfied with good quality dragon. Do *not* wish to exchange."

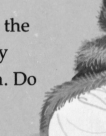

BUMBLYWITCH

At the bottom of Farmer Tumlytod's field, in a cottage shaped like a honeypot, there lived a witch. She was both good and kind and her name was Bumblywitch. Her black cat was called Jet and he had green eyes. He was fond of Bumblywitch and took care of her.

"Meow Maroo," he would say to Bumblywitch, "I am near you."

On a different patch, in cottages of their own, lived Bumblywitch's two sisters, Grumblywitch and Fumblywitch. They got on well together and often met for a talk.

Bumblywitch liked doing things to help people when they were ill or had a problem. "Izzy Whizzy, must keep busy," she was always saying. Nothing was ever too much trouble. A simple magic spell, a herb potion, these things kept her busy and the days passed happily.

The bees in the hive in her garden would hum bits of news in her ear, "Old Henry's hens are not laying. Granny Granger's goose is straying," they buzzed at her. Animals and birds often came to the cottage too, to tell Bumblywitch when there were things that needed her attention.

There was always plenty of work to do.

There came a day when Bumblywitch had a problem of her own, she was getting too fat! She gave Jet his saucer of milk, sat down to put on her elastic-sided witch's boots and found they would not go on! It was impossible!

"Oh Fiddledeedee," cried poor Bumblywitch, "I know I love doughnuts and chocolate when I get a sinking feeling inside me and I enjoy hot buttered toast when I'm sitting in my comfortable chair by the fire and cups of hot sweet tea. Oh dear, Jet, do you think I could wear my best buckle shoes?" and she went to fetch them.

Jet watched her carefully. "Meow Maroo," he said, and thought to himself that Bumblywitch was indeed *much* rounder than she used to be.

Bumblywitch sat down again and tried to put on her best witch's buckle shoes, but they hurt her ankles.

"Bumblyberries, I shall have to go out in my slippers because I must go and gather some more herbs," she cried. "Oh this is terrible!"

Hoping that she would not meet another witch while she was wearing her slippers, Bumblywitch went out. She walked to a nearby hedge to look for more herbs to fill up her store in the cottage. Bending with difficulty over a rather wide ditch, poor Bumblywitch slipped and fell in headfirst. The ditch was watery and rather unpleasant. Some pigeons who were in a tree watching, sang unkindly,

"Poor Bumblywitch,
She fell in a ditch,
Couldn't get out,
She stuck, 'cos she's stout!"

Then the pigeons felt sorry and wanted to help her. Flying down from their tree, they took hold of her clothes in their beaks and gently pulled her out. Muddy and very short of breath, Bumblywitch saw that her tall, black hat was stuck in the bottom of the ditch.

"Toads and Newts," she said loudly, feeling how it was very very improper for a witch to be seen wearing slippers and without a hat as well. Two kind crows pulled her hat out of the ditch and put it back on her head, although it was a bit wet! It dripped muddy water down her face.

"Whatever would my sisters say if they could see me now. Just as well they live on a different patch," gasped Bumblywitch. It was all so funny that she began to laugh. She thanked the birds for helping her and, walking very carefully, went back to her little cottage.

"Meow Maree," said Jet when he met her at the cottage door, "Meow Maroo, what did you do?" He was upset because if he had been there, perhaps he could have stopped Bumblywitch from falling in the watery ditch.

Bumblywitch made some tea and hot buttered toast and poured out a large saucer of milk for Jet. After he had finished his milk, in between washing and purring, Jet told Bumblywitch that Widow Twitchett's cow Daisy was sick. At once she got to her feet and went to fetch her broomstick because she did feel a little tired.

"I won't be long," she said to Jet, "a little magic whispered in Daisy's large, soft ear will soon put that right." She would take over some ointment for Widow Twitchett's bad knees too. Taking her broomstick into the yard outside, Bumblywitch put her leg over it and sat down, saying,

"Broomstick, broomstick,

Now I'm ready.

Travel me quick,

Keep me steady."

At once, the broomstick whirred into action for take-off. There was a strange noise, clouds of dust rose from underneath, the handle of the broomstick rose slightly, but Bumblywitch did not!

What was happening now! The broomstick was trying so hard to move but he simply could not rise from the ground. Bumblywitch was far too heavy. Very cross and not a little upset, Bumblywitch tried stronger magic,

"Rise I say, up and away.

On the ground you shall not stay."

The broomstick rose from the ground for about twelve inches, then with a very loud bump, returned to the ground again. It was no good. For once in her life, kind Bumblywitch was angry and with herself. This was too much. First her boots and now her broomstick.

"You are in no way to blame," she told her broomstick, "this is all my fault." As she put him away in his usual corner, she decided what she must do. She must act at once. She must get thinner and she must do it quickly before the other witches found out.

No more doughnuts, no more chocolate (except on Saturday night) less butter on her toast and only a small spoonful of honey in her nightly hot drink.

As she was unable to ride her broomstick, she would have to walk everywhere and work twice as hard. Now she must begin by walking over to Widow Twitchett and Daisy the cow.

"Hocus Pocus," said Bumblywitch as she walked up hill and down hill. Luckily for her, as she was a witch, she was able to use a little simple magic for getting over stiles and awkward places. Otherwise, Bumblywitch walked everywhere. Her good friend Farmer Tumlytod grew quite concerned about her. Returning to her cottage, Bumblywitch met him and he noticed how tired and out of breath she was. He offered to lend her his bicycle! She thanked him warmly because it was so very kind . . . . . but who ever heard of a witch riding a bicycle! The days passed and it was no laughing matter. "Meow Maroo," Jet said to Bumblywitch as he wound himself around her much thinner legs.

Imagine a witch who couldn't ride her broomstick or wear proper witch's boots and shoes with buckles. She had eaten less, walked more, worked harder and she did feel better.

"Now I shall try again," she told Jet, as she picked up her elastic-sided witch's boots.

"Meow, Meow, Maroo," said Jet watching Bumblywitch putting on her boots without any trouble at all.

Now for her dear, faithful broomstick. Bumblywitch carried him outside carefully; it was a long time since that dreadful day when she had been too heavy. Bumblywitch sat down very gently and said,

"Broomstick, broomstick,
Now I'm ready.
Travel me quick,
Keep me steady."

It was a magical moment; they rose in the air at once. 'I'm not so fat, I'm not so heavy' thought Bumblywitch, 'and indeed I never will be again. Plenty of exercise, not having a second helping and not being too quick to pop a piece of chocolate in my mouth. In future I will only ride my broomstick when it is necessary and walk at other times. It is really very easy if you put your mind to it.'

"Now we will go over to see my sisters," she told the broomstick. "We can tell each other our new spells"

It would be fun to see if they noticed that she was thinner. Last time she had seen them, Grumblywitch and Fumblywitch had cackled a little unkindly and said that her shadow was getting larger.

Whoops, the broomstick dipped and swerved quite alarmingly because Bumblywitch wasn't thinking. "I must pay more attention' she thought, 'after all we are a bit out of practice.'

"Heigho, away we go," said Bumblywitch to the broomstick, and setting a steady course, they sailed over the trees and vanished out of sight.

The Two Wizards

Once there were three brothers. The two eldest spent all their spare time playing draughts, and the youngest spent all his time learning how to become a wizard. One day, Bertram, who already knew a thing or two about wizardry, said, to his brothers,

"I feel like having some fun. I will change myself into a horse, and you can take me into the city and sell me."

"What will happen when you are sold?" asked his brothers.

"It will be fun to find out," said Bertram.

Who should buy Bertram in his new shape as a white horse, but the King himself. He paid for him with twelve of the best elephants in the palace elephant stable.

"What are you going to do?" whispered Bertram's brothers as the King prepared to mount. "The King will behead you if he finds out you have tricked him."

"Don't worry about me," whispered Bertram. "Take the elephants and go home."

The white horse gave the King a splendid ride. No one else could keep up with him. When they arrived at the palace gate the King had to dismount to open the gate himself.

No sooner had he dismounted than the white horse bolted.

"Catch that horse! Catch that horse!" shouted the King. But by the time the grooms had mounted their horses, the white horse was nowhere to be seen.

The King sent for his own wizard.

"I paid twelve of my best elephants for that horse," he said. "You MUST find it."

The King's wizard was no fool. He knew a thing or two himself. 'Set a horse to catch a horse,' he thought, and changed himself into a black stallion.

The white horse was grazing in a field. He heard the black stallion galloping towards him, and changed himself into a large white eagle. He soared up into the sky on strong white wings.

The King's wizard, who certainly did know a thing or two, changed into a black eagle. He soared up into the sky on strong black wings.

The white eagle saw him coming and changed into a white hawk. The black eagle changed into a black kite and chased the hawk into the trees, where Bertram's brothers were sitting playing draughts.

The white hawk changed into a white draught piece and hid amongst the other pieces on the board.

The black kite changed into the King's wizard.

"May I have my draught piece?" he asked.

"These are OUR draught pieces," said Bertram's brothers.

"Count them. You will find you have one too many," said the King's wizard. Of course, when Bertram's brothers counted the pieces, they found they did have one too many.

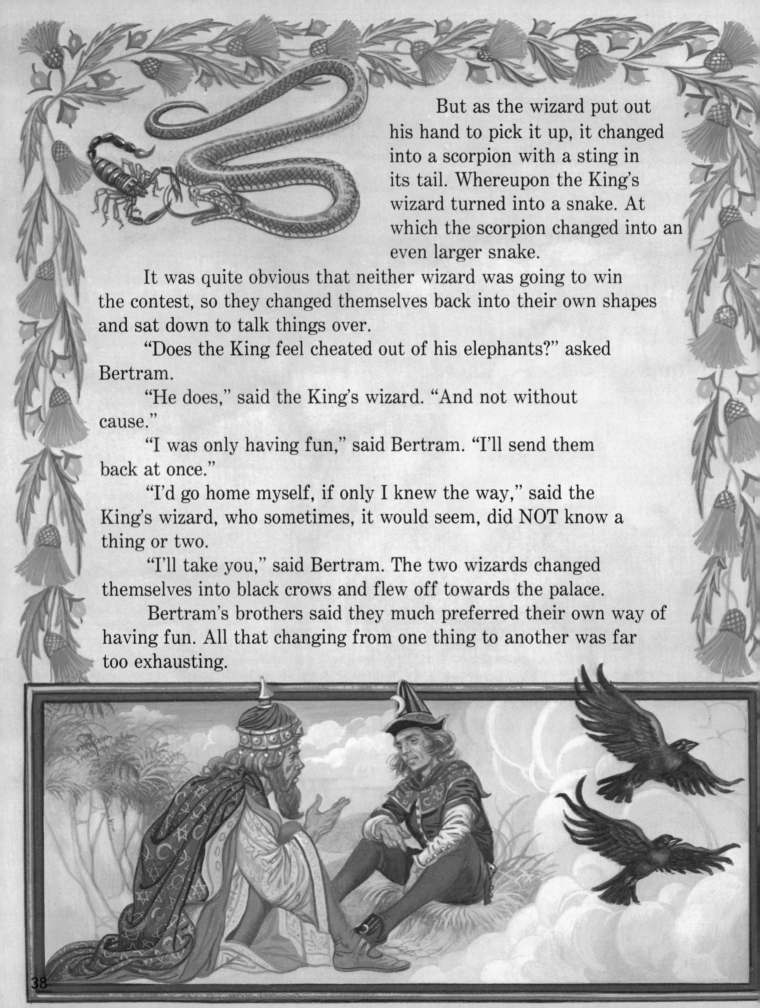

But as the wizard put out his hand to pick it up, it changed into a scorpion with a sting in its tail. Whereupon the King's wizard turned into a snake. At which the scorpion changed into an even larger snake.

It was quite obvious that neither wizard was going to win the contest, so they changed themselves back into their own shapes and sat down to talk things over.

"Does the King feel cheated out of his elephants?" asked Bertram.

"He does," said the King's wizard. "And not without cause."

"I was only having fun," said Bertram. "I'll send them back at once."

"I'd go home myself, if only I knew the way," said the King's wizard, who sometimes, it would seem, did NOT know a thing or two.

"I'll take you," said Bertram. The two wizards changed themselves into black crows and flew off towards the palace.

Bertram's brothers said they much preferred their own way of having fun. All that changing from one thing to another was far too exhausting.

French Puck

French Puck was very fond of playing tricks. He never did anyone harm, but he sometimes made people feel very foolish.

One day he overheard two people talking.

"It is our wedding day a week from tomorrow," said Jeanne. "It is market day today. We must go into town and buy all the things we need to set up house."

"There will be a lot to carry," said Jules. "We must take the horse and cart."

French Puck chuckled to himself, and sat on a fence and teased some chickens to while away the time while he waited for their return. With so many things to buy they were sure to forget something.

It was late afternoon before Jeanne and Jules returned. The cart was so loaded there was barely room for them on it.

French Puck leapt through the air, light as a goose feather, and sat on a chair leg behind them.

"Have we knives?" Jeanne was asking.

"Yes."

"Have we soap?"

"Yes."

"Then we have everything we need," said Jeanne with a happy sigh, and she snuggled up to Jules and began to dream about their wedding day.

The horse was trotting. The birds were singing. Jules was whistling. Jeanne was dreaming. And French Puck was waiting. He didn't have long to wait.

Suddenly, Jeanne sat up with such a start, Jules jerked on the horse's reins, and between them they almost upset the cart.

"Oh, no," wailed Jeanne.

A gleeful grin spread across French Puck's face. He rubbed his hands together in anticipation and his pointed ears twitched.

'Ho, ho,' he thought to himself. 'She's remembered something she has forgotten.'

"Whatever made you shout out like that?" asked Jules when they had quietened the horse and made sure nothing had fallen from the cart.

"I've forgotten to buy the thread the dressmaker needs to sew my wedding clothes," sighed Jeanne.

"Is THAT all! Surely you've got thread at home," said Jules.

"Only white . . . I need pink, and the palest of yellow, and apricot and delicate sky blue, and one with a touch of green in it. We shall have to go back to town to get some."

Jules sighed. It was a long way back to town, but he supposed he would have to go. He had the cart turned half way across the road when Jeanne cried out again.

"Look! Look!"

"What now?" grumbled Jules, who had quite enough to do trying to persuade the horse to take the right direction.

"Hey! Be careful!" he cried as Jeanne jumped from the cart.

"Look! A ball of thread!" And what a ball of thread it was! It had ALL the colours in it that she needed -- pink, yellow, apricot, sky blue and delicate green.

"Oh, what a lucky thing I saw it," cried Jeanne.

"But how did it get there?" asked Jules.

"This isn't the time to be asking silly questions," said Jeanne, climbing back onto the cart.

Jules turned the cart homewards again and they continued on their way, with Jeanne carrying the precious ball of thread on her lap, and with French Puck doing somersaults on the chair leg behind them.

The dressmaker was very pleased when she saw the thread. "It's absolutely perfect," she said. She was even more pleased with it as she sewed the wedding clothes. It was as smooth as silk, it didn't break, it didn't knot, and each colour was exactly the right length.

The wedding day came, and everyone, and that included French
Puck, gathered outside the church to see the new bride. How
pretty she looked.

"What a beautiful dress!" everybody exclaimed.

And then it happened! Crick! Crack! The tiny coloured
bows decorating the skirt began to float to the ground.

"Ooh!" gasped Jeanne.

"What is happening?" gasped everyone else.

Crick! Crack! The muslin flowers decorating the bodice
fell in a shower of petals.

Crick! Crack! The frill round the bottom of the skirt fell to the ground . . . then the skirt itself tumbled round Jeanne's ankles . . . the sleeves came apart and fell from her arms . . . the bodice fell into five different pieces.

Poor Jeanne was left standing in her petticoat, with her wedding dress in tatters around her. Someone ran from the crowd and put a cloak round her shoulders, and Jules took her home so that she could put on another dress.

"The thread I sewed with must have been rotten," said the dressmaker, who was blushing as scarlet as Jeanne herself. Oh, the shame of it all.

When everyone else had gone, she gathered the pieces together. She looked at them very carefully. She turned each piece over and over. She couldn't find one tiny piece of sewing thread anywhere. It had ALL disappeared.

"I should have known such perfect thread was too good to be true," she sighed.

The mystery was never explained, but then nobody had seen French Puck, had they?

The Magic Pot

Once upon a time, there was a girl who lived with her mother in a tiny house on the outskirts of a small town. They were very poor and sometimes they were very hungry. They often had nothing to eat at all.

One day, when the girl was out in the woods searching for mushrooms and blackberries, she met an old woman who was carrying an empty iron pot.

"Take it," said the old woman putting the pot into her hands. "When you are hungry, say to it 'Little pot boil'. When you have enough, say, 'Little pot stop'."

The girl thought it very strange, but she took the pot home and told her mother what the old woman had said.

"Put it on the table, say the words, and we will see what happens," said her mother.

"Little pot boil," said the girl. Hardly were the words spoken than the pot began to bubble and hiss, and steam began to rise from it.

"It's filling up," gasped the girl.

"It's truly a magic pot," said her mother. "Stop it before it overflows."

"Little pot stop," said the girl. The bubbling and hissing stopped at once. "What a delicious smell," said the girl.

"That looks and smells very like porridge to me," said her mother. "Bring two plates and two spoons and we will taste it."

It was the sweetest, creamiest, nicest porridge either of them had ever tasted. And with a magic porridge pot like that at their command, their days of being hungry were over. It didn't matter how much porridge they ate, there was always some more to be had at the command 'Little pot boil'.

One day, when the girl was out, her mother set the pot on the table, and said, "Little pot boil". The bubbling began, the steam began to rise, the delicious smell of porridge began to fill the room. The sweet, creamy porridge reached the brim of the pot. The girl's mother opened her mouth to say the words to stop it and found she couldn't remember them. All she could think to say was, "Um er . . . that's enough". A tiny trickle of porridge began to run down the OUTSIDE of the porridge pot. The pot had never done that before. "Stop . . . stop . . ." she shouted in a panic. "I don't want any more . . . stop filling up . . . go away . . ." The harder she tried to remember the right words the worse it became.

The pot bubbled and bubbled. The trickle of porridge became a stream. It spread across the table and fell in a sticky cascade to the floor.

"Whatever shall I do?" she wailed as she climbed onto a chair. "Please . . . please . . . please stop . . . please pot!"

The pool of porridge spread to the door and ran out into the street.

"Stop! . . Stop! . ." she shouted. "Come back porridge . . . get back into the pot . . . please stop! . ." The porridge pot took no notice. It would only stop when it was given the right command. But what WAS the right command?

The sweet creamy porridge began to behave like an overflowing river. It ran on and on along the streets, into the houses and the dog kennels. It filled up the fish ponds and the drains.

"What's happening?" shouted the citizens of the town as they took off their shoes and waded through the sticky mess.

"It's the pot . . . it won't stop," cried the girl's mother.

The citizens began to shout commands then. The dogs began to bark and the cats began to miaow.

"Stop making porridge before we all drown . . . Stop! . . Stop! . ."

The girl was visiting at the far edge of the town. She heard the commotion and looked out of the window to see what the noise was about. As soon as she saw the rivers of porridge oozing through the streets she guessed at once what had happened. She ran home as fast as the sticky porridge would let her.

"Do something, do something quickly!" urged the townsfolk. When she got home her mother was still shouting commands at the pot. "Stop cooking . . . stop bubbling . . . Stop! . . Stop! . ."

"Little pot stop!" said the girl. THAT was the right command and the pot DID stop. Instantly.

"I'll only use the pot when you are here in future," said her mother. "I don't want that to happen again."

Neither did anyone else. It took ages to clean up the town and no one wants to do that kind of sticky job twice.

The New Coat

One day, when the sun was shining, Mr. Mole popped his head out of his hole and said, "Where's this water coming from? I'm getting flooded out of my home."

"Whoo, whoo, it's the Gentle Giant," called the Owl. "He is crying so much that he has washed me off my branch."

"I was having such a lovely sleep. Whatever can be the matter with him?"

"I'll go and find out," said the Squirrel. Away he ran, up and up from one branch to another, up the tallest tree until he reached the topmost branch. The branch swayed to and fro in the breeze, so he had to cling on very tightly with his claws. He said to his friend, the Giant, "Why are you so sad? What is making you cry like this?"

"I am so cold," said the Giant, shivering and making all the trees rustle as he did so. "I haven't got a warm coat."

The Squirrel scampered down the tree and gathered all the animals around him, to tell them how unhappy and cold the Giant had become.

"We must do something before the snow comes," said Mrs. Rabbit. All was quiet as everyone tried to think of a way out of the problem.

"We could plait the long reeds that grow down by the river," suggested the Fox. "We could collect all the down from the thistles, and make it nice and warm," cried the field mice. They ran around in circles because they were so excited to be helping to make the coat.

So, using sharp thorns for needles and fine grass for the thread, they started to sew. All through the day, the animals took it in turns because it was very tiring. You see, they were so small and the coat had to be so big.

Again the Squirrel ran up the tall tree to tell his friend the Gentle Giant all about his new coat. "It won't take us very long," said the Squirrel. "Everyone is busy and working very hard."

"Oh, thank you," cried the Giant. "You are very kind. I just don't know how I can repay you."

When the coat was almost finished, the wise old Owl said, "How are you going to get the coat up to the Giant when it is ready? It looks very heavy to me. If the Giant bends down he will break all our lovely trees."

"Oh dear, oh dear," said the animals. "Whatever shall we do?"

All of a sudden, the trees were filled with birdsong. From every tree birds swooped down—big ones, small ones, plain ones and pretty ones.

"We'll do it," they sang. "We could not help to make the coat, but we can take it to him for you."

When it was ready, the birds lifted the coat high into the air and held it up for the Giant while he wrapped himself in its warm folds.

"You look after us, so we will look after you," sang the birds. The Giant was so grateful for his present that he took extra care of the little wood where so many of his friends lived.

FELIX THE MAGICIAN

Long, long ago there lived a good and clever magician whose name was Felix. He lived on the border between two warlike countries. Felix knew that King Lofty on the one side and King Trump on the other were jealous of each other and needed little excuse to start a war.

Their armies trained by marching up hill and down dale all day long. Tramp, tramp, tramp.

Felix was cross.

"I must put a stop to it," he said to himself. But how?

Felix thought and thought. He even worried about it in his sleep.

"At last," he cried, jumping out of bed one night in his night-shirt and cap.

He searched through his spell books until he found what he was looking for, then he carried it upstairs with him and sat up in bed reading it carefully. Every now and then, he nodded and chuckled to himself, and at last, he lay down and went fast asleep.

Felix spent all the next day preparing and just before midnight he left the house making his way to the border. Luckily there was very little moonlight, but he had to go carefully not to be seen by one of the soldiers.

First, he stood facing one way and held up his arms chanting very quietly to himself. He turned and did the same thing facing the other way. Then he jumped smartly to one side and made his way home chuckling to himself.

The following morning he found he had just been in time. The soldiers were preparing themselves for battle. Rank upon rank were lined up facing each other. Felix was not smiling now. Thinking of all the dreadful things that would have happened if he had not cast his spell made him very angry.

On one side of the border, King Lofty stood near his white horse his captains grouped about him.

King Trump was already astride his black horse waiting for his officers to tell him they were ready.

There were only a few yards between the armies, but when Felix thought of those few yards he had to smile. He went out and sat on a large rock where he could see everything that was going on. He did not want to miss anything.

Felix had to admit they looked a wonderful sight lined up facing each other. The soldiers stood in ranks, their spears and shields glinting in the sun. Behind them the archers stood, their bows and arrows ready.

Now, both kings held their swords aloft ready to give a signal. Both arms came down almost at the same moment. The two armies marched towards each other, shields in place and spears ready. Both sides thrust their spears forward but they did not touch the men on the other side. Instead they buckled and snapped in half! The soldiers fell backwards in a heap. The same thing happened to the next rank and the one after.

By now the archers had started to let fly their arrows. These flew only so far in the air then fell harmlessly to the ground. Felix was enjoying himself, he laughed until the tears ran down his cheeks.

Some of the archers began to smile, then laugh; they could not help it. It was such a funny sight – all those arms and legs waving in the air.

King Lofty and King Trump looked stupidly at their men who kept marching forward and falling on top of the soldiers already on the ground. The laughter spread until even the two kings had to join in. At last, one of the officers gave the command to halt.

Felix waved his arms to take the invisible wall away. One of the soldiers noticed Felix sitting on the rock, and pointed to him. Everybody became silent looking towards him. King Lofty and King Trump rode up to him and dismounted. Seeing his hat and cloak they looked at each other.

"You did this," said King Lofty.

"Why?" asked King Trump.

"Yes, it was me," said Felix. "Why? Well, someone had to do something before you destroyed each other."

"How did you do it?" asked King Lofty.

"It was simple really,' said Felix. "I put an invisible wall between you."

Well, the kings were very impressed and said how clever he had been.

"Yes, I know that," said Felix modestly. "Come now," he went on.

"Shake hands and forget this war. It seems to me that you are both to blame."

The two kings looked at each other. Then they smiled and clasped hands. The soldiers cheered their kings, the officers and most of all Felix, the clever magician.

Felix was delighted his spell had worked. He invited both kings and their officers to his house to rest and talk. All the men of both sides joined together, laughing and clapping each other on the back.

Felix waved his arms, and food and drink appeared by magic. The men cheered once more, then they ate and drank until it was almost dark, before going home. There was so much to tell their families, they could hardly believe all the wonderful things that had happened that day.

Felix's name was on everyone's lips, and he was blessed that day and for many, many years to come.

The White Dove

Once, on a cold and blustery day, a coach was travelling through the forest. It was bumping along over the ruts and through the puddles when a band of robbers ran from the trees.

"Your money or your lives!" they shouted.

As the coachman pulled hard on the reins, and the coach came to a halt, one of the doors jolted open. A slim girl, with brown hair, managed to slip unnoticed through the door and into the trees. She ran deeper and deeper into the forest, catching her dress on brambles and losing her shoes as she went. She did not stop running until the shouts of the robbers had faded away into the distance and all she could hear were the birds. And then, she sat on a fallen log, and buried her face in her hands. She was safe from the robbers it was true, but she was alone in a deep dark wood, with nowhere to go, and no one to help her.

"Oh woe is me," she sobbed. "What shall I do? I will never find my way out of the forest."

Presently, through her sobs, she heard the gentle whirr of wings. She looked up and saw a white dove hovering in front of her. It was carrying a tiny key in its beak. It dropped the key on the moss at her feet, and said,

"In the tree behind you, you will find a tiny lock. Open it with the key."

Sure enough, hidden in the bark of the tree, and so tiny that she almost missed it, was a tiny keyhole. She turned the key in it and a door opened to reveal a cupboard containing bread, and milk.

"Thank you little dove," said the girl, through her tears.

When she had eaten, the dove dropped a second key at her feet. That opened a tree door which led to a room just large enough to hold a bed.

"Sleep there, and you will be safe," said the dove.

The days passed, and whenever the girl was in need of anything the dove came to her with a key which opened yet another door in yet another tree. One day, when the dove was sitting on her hand, it said, "Will you do something for me?"

"Gladly," said the girl, stroking the dove's soft feathers.

"Then listen carefully," said the dove. "Follow the path that leads into the deepest part of the wood. It will lead you to a cottage. In the cottage you will see an old woman sitting by the fire. Do not speak to her but pass on her right side and enter the room behind her. On the table you will see many rings encrusted with jewels that sparkle like fire, and amongst them, one made of gold. Please bring me the gold ring."

The girl followed the path and found the cottage. She could see the old woman sitting by the fire.

"What are you doing?" croaked the old woman, as the girl crept past her. The girl put her hand over her mouth so that she would not be tricked into speaking. She found the table covered with jewelled rings, but of the golden ring there was no sign. And then she saw the old woman sneaking through the door with a bird-cage hidden under her shawl.

'The ring must be in the cage' thought the girl, and snatched it from the old woman. Sure enough, the bird was holding the ring in its beak. The girl took it gently, and then ran to the tree where her friend the dove had told her to wait. The dove was not there. She waited, and waited, and still the dove did not come. She leant sadly against the tree, and her tears began to fall as she thought perhaps she would never see the dove again. And then, something very strange happened. The tree felt strangely soft, for a tree . . . and then, it seemed to grow arms which wrapped themselves around her.

''Do not cry,'' said a gentle voice.

The tree was changing into a prince, and all around her other trees were changing into the prince's friends.

''Do not be afraid,'' said the Prince, for of course, the girl WAS afraid. ''The woman in the cottage is a witch. She cast a spell on us all. She turned us into trees, but because I am a prince she allowed me to fly as a dove, for two hours every day.''

He gently uncurled the girl's fingers and took the ring from her hand. ''When you took this from the witch you broke her spell.''

And then the girl recognized the voice of her dear friend the dove, and she was afraid no longer.

Like most fairy stories, this one has a happy ending too. The girl married the prince and became a princess, and they lived happily ever after.

GLUM THE GIANT

Glum, the Giant, strode along the road away from the village with his bag on his shoulder. He had been shopping. Several people smiled at him but he only nodded back at them. They took no notice, they were used to him.

Then some children followed him chanting,
"There goes poor old Glum,
He has a pain in his tum.
Oh, why does he scowl?
He should be called Growl."

Glum spun round and glared at them. They ran away laughing, as they knew he would not harm them.

Glum went on his way thinking hard. What was the matter with him? Why couldn't he smile and laugh like other people? Perhaps if he tried it would help. How did they smile? They showed their teeth, didn't they? Glum thought he would try out his idea of a smile on the next person he saw.

The giant went on his way until he saw a boy on a horse coming towards him.

"Hello Glum," called the boy. Glum remembered his idea and smiled. At least he thought it was a smile, but it frightened the horse so much that it reared up and bolted almost unseating the boy.

Glum dropped his bag and took only a few strides to catch the horse by the reins, just in time.

"Whoa there," Glum said gently stroking the horse's nose with one finger while he helped the boy to sit up straight. The horse stopped trembling and neighed as if in answer.

"Are you alright, boy?" he asked.

"Yes, thank you," was the rather shaky answer.

"Well, take it easy then, goodbye."

Glum left the boy wondering what could have happened for the giant to pull such a funny face.

Glum came to a large pond where a lot of ducks and fish lived. He leaned over to look into the water but his shadow was so dark that he could not see himself.

Glum still did not know what he looked like.

He carried on until he came to his gloomy old castle and went in slamming the door behind him.

Glum looked about him and seemed to see everything with new eyes. He had never noticed before that the dark grey walls were hanging with cobwebs, or that the floor was so dirty and the furniture thick with dust. He had no one to look after him, it was true.

"That is no excuse," Glum told himself, suddenly upset with the state the place was in.

"I ought to look for a wife, but who would have me? If the castle has to be cleaned I will have to do it myself."

He made himself some supper and went to bed feeling more glum than ever.

That night he had a strange dream. He was a handsome giant who had rescued a fair young giantess from the clutches of her wicked uncle. When he woke he remembered his dream and thought sadly how lonely he was.

"Come on," he reminded himself. "There is work to be done."

All day long he swept, dusted and polished the old castle. Clouds of dust flew out of the doors and all the windows. The people in the village some distance away wondered what on earth was happening.

By the time Glum had finished, the castle looked a different place but he himself was a mess; not that he ever looked very tidy but now he was dirty as well.

He picked up a large bar of soap and a towel as big as a blanket and made his way to the river nearby.

First, he took off his boots, emptied the dust out of them, then polished them with his sleeve until they shone. Then he waded into the river as he was, with his clothes on and sat in the middle of it.

"Ah," he sighed. "That feels nice and cool after all my hard work."

Glum bent forward to splash himself with water, holding the soap in one hand. He stared at the face looking back at him for a few moments, then he began to roar with peals of laughter. He laughed and laughed until the tears rolled down his cheeks.

At last, still chuckling, he looked up to see the people from the village standing on the bank watching him in amazement.

"Are you alright?" one of the men asked him.

Glum laughed again.

"I've just seen the funniest face looking up at me from the river," he explained. "It is the first time I have seen something that made me want to laugh. I do feel good now. I can understand at last why people like to smile and feel happy."

"That was your own face in the water," one little boy said before they could stop him.

"My own face?" Glum sounded astonished. He looked again into the water and saw himself once more.

"Well," he said at last. "If that is what I look like, no wonder I am called Glum."

He put his head under the water and gave himself a good scrub, clothes and all. Then he stood up and shook himself before reaching for his towel.

"I can cut your hair and trim your beard if you would like me to," the barber dared to say.

"Why, that is most kind of you," Glum said smiling at him.

They all smiled back.

"No time like the present," the barber said, taking comb and scissors from his pocket.

When he had finished, everybody stared at Glum.

"There, that has made a difference, hasn't it?" said the barber.

Glum leaned over and looked at himself in the river. He turned his head from side to side, putting his hand up to feel his beard. Then he smiled and at last he laughed showing his white teeth. His hair and beard were brown and his eyes deep blue.

"Is that really me?" he asked.

"Yes, indeed it is," an old lady answered. "If I may say so, you are a very handsome giant now."

Glum rose to his feet and bowed low to her. "Thank you, my lady," he chuckled.

Everybody clapped and laughed. The children danced around him singing,

"Oh me, oh my, what a handsome guy,

He will make all the ladies sigh."

Then Glum thought, maybe some day, his dream might not be so impossible after all.

THE MAGIC COMBS

"King Bonkers may be my father," said Princess Mirabelle, as she brushed the mud from the coat of her little dog, "but I think he must be the silliest King that ever lived."

"King Bonkers may be my husband," said the Queen as she pruned her favourite rose bush, "but I have to agree with you. If he isn't complaining how bored he is, he is playing silly tricks on people. Everybody is tired of him and if he doesn't mend his ways soon, the people will choose a new King and we shall all be turned out of our beautiful palace."

King Bonkers walked across the lawn towards the Queen and Princess.

"I am so bored," he said.

"We could all be bored if we walked around all day doing nothing," said the Queen. "Have you signed your important papers today?"

"No," answered King Bonkers. "Important papers bore me."

"Well, you could help me prune the roses," suggested the Queen.

"No thank you," said King Bonkers, "I might prick my fingers." And he walked out of the palace gate and up the hill to Wizard Winegum's house.

Wizard Winegum wasn't very pleased to see King Bonkers.

"Tell me what you want quickly," he said. "I am very busy today."

"I am bored," said King Bonkers, "and I want a spell to make something exciting happen."

Wizard Winegum stroked his long white beard thoughtfully.

"Well hm, well hm, I have some magic combs," he said. "If you comb your hair with one of these combs, everything you touch for half an hour afterwards will turn into something different."

"Into what?" asked King Bonkers.

"That's the trouble," answered Wizard Winegum. "You won't know until you touch it. The combs are quite expensive. Twenty gold pieces each."

"I will take two," said King Bonkers and he counted out forty gold pieces.

"Are you quite sure you want two?" asked Wizard Winegum, taking the combs down from his high shelf. "Surely one will be enough?"

"I want two," said King Bonkers and he took the combs and ran back to the palace as fast as his little fat legs would carry him.

Puffing and panting he ran up the stairs to the Queen's bedroom. The Queen was sitting at her dressing table brushing her hair.

"I have bought you a nice new comb, dear," said King Bonkers handing her one of the combs.

"Oh thank you, that is kind of you," she said and she combed her hair with the magic comb. She then put the comb down and picked up her hair brush.

As soon as she touched it, the brush turned into a spider. The Queen hated spiders. She screamed and dropped the spider. It fell onto her lap.

She tried to knock the spider from her lap onto the floor but as she touched it, it turned into a mouse. The Queen was terrified of mice. She climbed onto a chair screaming to King Bonkers to take the mouse away.

As she touched the chair it turned into a kangaroo. It hopped out of the door with the Queen clinging to its neck.

King Bonkers thought this was very funny and laughed and laughed until the tears ran down his fat cheeks.

Still laughing, King Bonkers went to give the other comb to Princess Mirabelle. The princess was playing with her little dog on her bedroom floor. King Bonkers handed her the comb.

"Oh thank you, father," she said, and combed her hair with the new comb.

She picked up a slide to put in her hair. At once the slide turned into a ginger kitten. The ginger kitten scratched her and wriggled out of her hands. It ran through the bedroom door and down the stairs chased by the princess's little dog.

Princess Mirabelle ran to the door to call her dog back. As she touched the door it turned into a horse. The horse ran down the stairs after the dog and the kitten.

Soon the whole palace was in an uproar with the kangaroo, dog, horse, kitten and mouse all chasing each other.

King Bonkers hadn't had so much fun for years. He laughed and laughed until he thought his sides would burst.

The next morning, King Bonkers left the palace bright and early to buy two more magic combs from Wizard Winegum.

Princess Mirabelle watched him from her bedroom window. She felt sure he was up to no good and had something to do with what had happened the day before. She decided to follow him.

She crouched down outside Wizard Winegum's door and listened through the keyhole as King Bonkers told the Wizard how pleased he had been with the combs and that he wanted to buy two more.

Princess Mirabelle ran back to the palace and told the Queen all she had overheard.

The Queen was very angry. "King Bonkers needs to be taught a lesson he will not forget in a hurry," she said. She bent down and whispered something in Princess Mirabelle's ear.

Princess Mirabelle smiled as she and the Queen went into the bedroom. They both sat down in front of the Queen's dressing table and started to brush their hair.

King Bonkers was very pleased to see them together when he entered the bedroom. It would save him a walk. He gave them a comb each and sat down on the Queen's bed to wait for the fun to begin.

After thanking him politely, the Queen and the Princess combed their hair with the magic combs AND THEN stood up together and walked slowly over to King Bonkers. The Queen put out her hand and touched King Bonkers on the top of his bald head.

King Bonkers turned into a big, fat round ball.

"Oh look!" said the Queen to Princess Mirabelle. "What a pretty ball. Throw it out of the window and see how well it bounces."

"Oh NO NO NO. I'm not a ball I'm ME!" shouted King Bonkers, but the Queen and the Princess pretended not to hear him.

Princess Mirabelle picked up the ball and at once the King turned into a frog.

"What a horrid frog," said the Queen. "Give it to me and I will put it in the fish pond."

"No, no. I'm not a frog, please don't put me in the fish pond. I can't swim," pleaded the King.

Between them the Queen and Princess Mirabelle soon turned King Bonkers into so many different things he felt quite giddy.

At last he turned into a little bird and flew out of the window and hid himself in a large oak tree.

"Oh dear, oh dear," he said. "I am so dizzy with all this changing. I haven't enjoyed it at all. I will never again use magic to play silly tricks on people." As he spoke, King Bonkers turned back into a King once more. He was a very fat king so it took him a long time to climb down from the tree.

"Oh dear, oh dear," he thought. "I do hope nobody sees me. It is so undignified for a *King* to have to climb down from a tree."

On reaching the ground he looked carefully around but fortunately no one was in sight. Full of his new resolve, he quickly returned to the palace and it wasn't long before he was renowned for his wisdom and good sense.

Thumbling

Once upon a time, there was a man who had a son no bigger than his thumb. He called him Thumbling and taught him how to cut and sew cloth, and how to look after himself, and not get caught by the cat or fall down a mouse-hole. Though he was so tiny, Thumbling was as brave and as bold as any other boy and just as mischievous. He had many adventures.

One day, Thumbling said to his father, "Father, I want to see something of the world."

"And so you shall my son," said Thumbling's father. He knew Thumbling would only sigh loudly and sew big uneven stitches until he had his way. The sooner he went and saw the world, the sooner he would come back home and help with the sewing.

He made Thumbling a sword from a darning needle and a knob of red wax and he made him a belt from button thread so that he could buckle the sword round his waist.

Thumbling's mother was cooking at the fireplace.

"That smells good," said Thumbling. "I'll have some of that before I go." He leant over the pot to sniff the delicious aroma of cooking lentils.

"Come back at once and say goodbye properly," grumbled his mother, as the steam from the cooking pot picked Thumbling up and wafted him up the chimney.

"Bye . . ." called Thumbling as he sailed away like a feather. "This is the only way to travel."

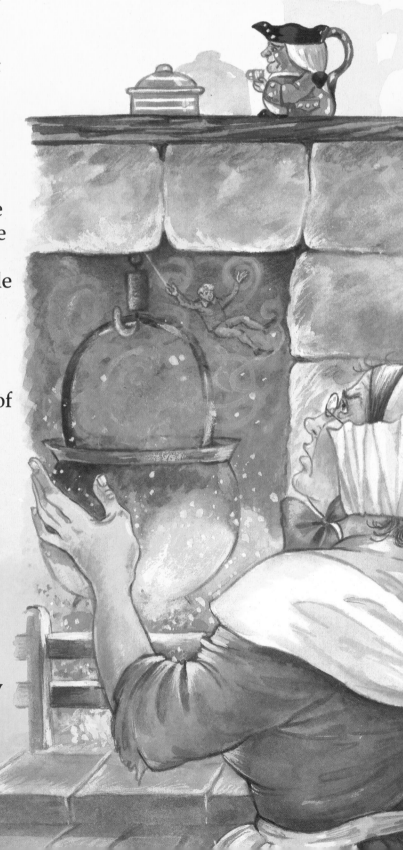

He finally sank to the ground on the far side of the valley. He found work with a man who was a tailor like his father. For a while Thumbling behaved himself, but he began to miss his mother's cooking. The tailor's wife was always forgetting to put the meat in the cooking pot and was always boiling the potatoes dry.

"One day," he said teasingly, "I shall go away if you don't feed me better and before I do, I will write on your door, 'Too many burnt potatoes and not enough meat'."

The tailor's wife was very cross. After all, she always did her best. She couldn't help it if the cooking went wrong sometimes.

"You little . . . grasshopper," she snapped and she picked up the dishcloth and tried to hit him with it.

"Ho . . ho . . can't catch me!" teased Thumbling, dodging out of the way with the greatest of ease. It is easy to dodge when you are small and easy to hide under a thimble.

"Here I am," he called to make sure she was looking his way, and when he saw she was, he poked out his tongue.

"You naughty little grasshopper . . ." she scolded as she lifted the thimble. "But I've caught you now."

"Oh no, you haven't," laughed Thumbling and he ran along the folds in the tablecloth playing hide and seek with her.

The tailor's wife caught hold of the corner of the cloth and pulled it to the floor. What a noise there was as the plates crashed and the knives clattered.

"Can't catch me!" sang Thumbling and jumped down into a crack in the table. He unbuckled his darning needle sword and every time the tailor's wife moved her hand towards him he pricked her thumb with it.

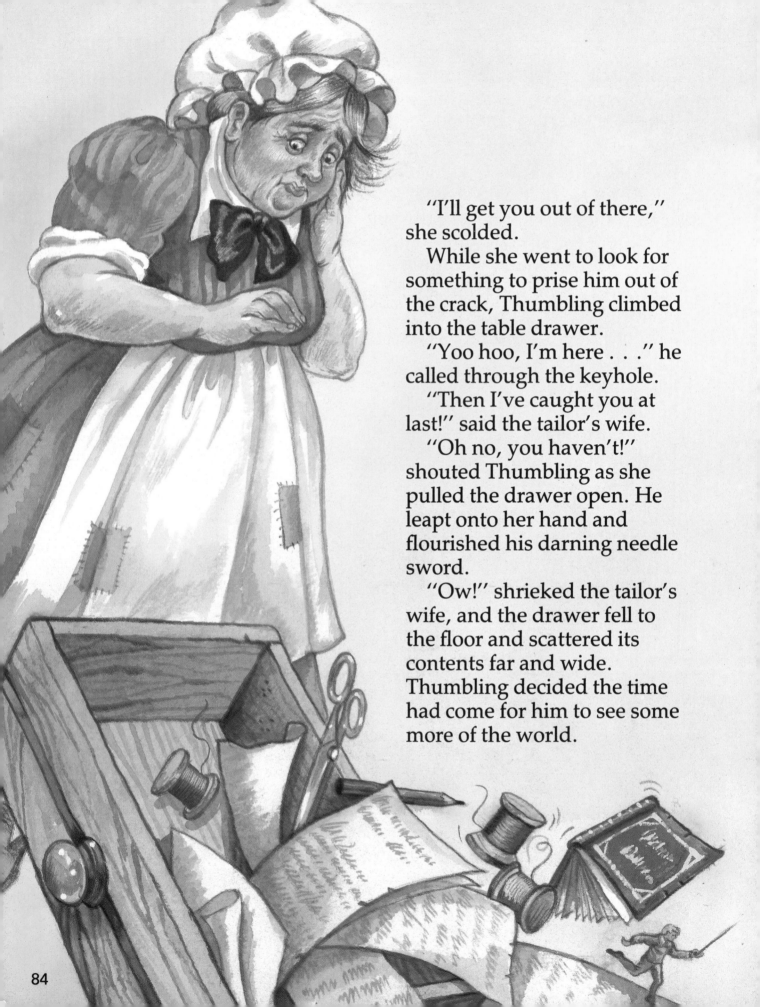

"I'll get you out of there," she scolded.

While she went to look for something to prise him out of the crack, Thumbling climbed into the table drawer.

"Yoo hoo, I'm here . . ." he called through the keyhole.

"Then I've caught you at last!" said the tailor's wife.

"Oh no, you haven't!" shouted Thumbling as she pulled the drawer open. He leapt onto her hand and flourished his darning needle sword.

"Ow!" shrieked the tailor's wife, and the drawer fell to the floor and scattered its contents far and wide. Thumbling decided the time had come for him to see some more of the world.

"Bye!" he called as he hopped, skipped and jumped along the path. "I'll leave you to clear away the mess."

"Away with you!" shouted the tailor's wife. "I would rather have a hive full of bees in my house than you." And with that she slammed the door and Thumbling went on his way.

THE HOUSE THAT JACK BUILT

This is the house that Jack built.

This is the tree
As you can see
That grew through the floor
And what is more
Grew right through the house that Jack built.

This is the rook
That came to look
To build his nest
His first and best
Up in the tree
As you can see
That grew through the floor
And what is more
Grew right through the house that Jack built.

This is his wife
Who shares his life
High in the nest
His first and best
Up in the tree
As you can see
That grew through the floor
And what is more
Grew right through the house that Jack built.

Here are their eggs
Safe in the nest
Their first and best
Up in the tree
As you can see
That grew through the floor
And what is more
Grew right through the house that Jack built.

"Our babies are hungry!"
   Mother Rook sings;
So, Father brings meals –
How happy he feels
And proud of his wife
Who shares his life
High in the nest
His first and best
Up in the tree
As you can see
That grew through the floor
And what is more
Grew right through the house that Jack built.

Caws never cease
As rooks increase
A real busy sound
And babies abound
Each from an egg
Their mouths all beg;
Husbands help wives
Who share their lives
High in each nest
Their first and best
Up in the tree
As you can see
That grew through the floor
And what is more
Grew right through the house that Jack built.

Jack calls his house
'The Rookery-Nook'
It's famous and so
He's writing a book.
Folks come by car
They come by plane;
They see it once
Then come again.
If the tree grows bigger,
Somebody said,
You'll never climb
Those stairs to bed!
Cut it down now!
That is the best!
'Good gracious!' thought Jack,
'And spoil each nest!
Never! No, never!
Not on your life!
I'll search and find
Myself a wife;
We'll stay right here
High up in the house that Jack built.'

Now Jack has a 'nest'
His first and best
He is happy
As happy can be
There with his wife
Who shares his life
High up in the tree
As you can see
That grew through the floor
And what is more
Grew right through the house that Jack built.

90

Chicken Licken

One morning, when Chicken Licken was sitting under an oak tree, an acorn fell upon his head.

"Oh dear," he gasped, "The sky is falling. I must run and tell the King."

On the way to the palace he met his friend Henny Penny.

"Where are you going?" asked Henny Penny.

"To tell the King the sky is falling," said Chicken Licken.

"Then I'll come with you," clucked Henny Penny.

Cocky Locky was scratching for grain.

"Where are you both going in such a hurry?" he asked.

"To tell the King the sky is falling," said Chicken Licken.

"Then I'll come with you," crowed Cocky Locky.

"Where are you all going?" asked Ducky Lucky, when she met them hurrying along a footpath.

"To tell the King the sky is falling," said Chicken Licken without stopping.

"Then I'll come with you," quacked Ducky Lucky.

"Where are you all going?" called Drakey Lakey from the pond.

"To tell the King the sky is falling," said Chicken Licken.

"Then I'll come with you," said Drakey Lakey shaking the water from his webbed feet.

Goosey Loosey was as anxious as everyone else to help tell the King the bad news.

"I'll come with you," she hissed as she stretched her long white neck.

"And I'll come too . . . too . . . too . . ." gobbled Turkey Lurkey who didn't like to be left out of anything.

Foxy Loxy was lurking behind a bush.

"Where are you all going in such a hurry?" he asked slyly.

"To tell the King the sky is falling," said Chicken Licken.

"Then you had better follow me," said Foxy Loxy. "I know of a short cut."

And he led Chicken Licken, Henny Penny, Cocky Locky, Ducky Lucky, Drakey Lakey, Goosey Loosey and Turkey Lurkey through the bushes to his den, where his wife and five hungry children were waiting.

And that, I am sorry to say, was the end of Chicken Licken, Henny Penny, Cocky Locky, Ducky Lucky, Drakey Lakey, Goosey Loosey and Turkey Lurkey, for the fox family had them for dinner, and the King never did find out that a piece of sky had fallen on Chicken Licken's head.

A Running Race

It was Sunday morning. Mrs. Hedgehog was busy in her kitchen and the Hedgehog children were playing hide and seek in the garden.

"I'm just going to the field to look at my turnips," called Mr. Hedgehog who liked a walk on Sunday mornings. He was half way there when he met Mr. Hare, who was also out walking.

Mr. Hare was going to look at his cabbages.

"Good morning," said Mr. Hedgehog in his usual polite and friendly manner. "Nice morning for a walk, isn't it?"

Mr. Hare stuck his nose in the air. "What does someone with legs as short as yours know about walking?" he said scornfully.

Mr. Hedgehog didn't like other animals making fun of his short legs.

"My legs are every bit as good as yours," he said.

"Fiddle-de-dee!" scoffed Mr. Hare. "That's nonsense and you know it. Why, I can outrun you any day."

"We will put it to the test," said Mr. Hedgehog. "I will wager you a cabbage to a turnip that I can run faster than *you*."

"What a ridiculous little hedgehog you are," said Mr. Hare. "But if you will insist on making yourself look foolish why should I stop you. Shall we begin?"

"I haven't had my breakfast yet," said Mr. Hedgehog. "I can't run on an empty stomach. I'll meet you in the big field in half an hour. We will run our race along the furrows."

"Very well," said Mr. Hare and went to get some breakfast himself.

"Quick wife! Quick!" said Mr. Hedgehog when he got home. "Take off your apron and come with me."

Of course Mrs. Hedgehog, who was so like Mr. Hedgehog that they looked like two peas from the same pod, wanted to know what the fuss was about. When Mr. Hedgehog told her she said Mr. Hare was quite right, he was silly.

"No hedgehog can run faster than a hare," she said. Little did she know Mr. Hedgehog had a plan and he needed her help. They reached the far end of the field, where the race was to be

run, while Mr. Hare was still eating his breakfast.

"Hide in that furrow wife," said Mr. Hedgehog. "When you hear me call 'I am here already' bob up your head and wave."

Mrs. Hedgehog didn't understand *why* she should do such a thing, but she agreed to do it all the same. When Mr. Hare arrived Mr. Hedgehog was waiting at the opposite end of the field.

"I'm ready," said Mr. Hedgehog. "Are you?"

Mr. Hare sniffed. He would show this silly hedgehog a thing or two. "Of course I'm ready," he said.

"Ready! Steady! GO!"

THEY WERE OFF!

Mr. Hare lolloped along, not really bothering to hurry. The furrows were deep and he couldn't see Mr. Hedgehog but he knew he had nothing to worry about. The turnip was as good as his. His legs were made for running. Mr. Hedgehog's were not.

He couldn't believe his ears when he got to the far end of the field and heard Mr. Hedgehog call "I am here already", or his eyes, when he saw a hedgehog head pop up from the furrow next to his. How was he to know that although he had heard Mr. Hedgehog, he was seeing *Mrs.* Hedgehog? 'I'll have to run faster on the way back,' he thought.

But just before he reached the end of the furrow Mr. Hedgehog popped up at the end of his furrow. And what was more, he wasn't even panting.

"It looks as though I have won," said Mr. Hedgehog.

How was Mr. Hare to know that Mr. Hedgehog had been crouching in the furrow and hadn't run at all?

"Let us race again," said Mr. Hare, convinced there had been a mistake. A hedgehog *cannot* run faster than a hare. Everyone knows that.

Mr. Hedgehog was only too glad to oblige.

Every time Mr. Hare reached the far edge of the field, Mr. Hedgehog called out "I am here already" and Mr. Hare would see *Mrs.* Hedgehog and think he was seeing *Mr.* Hedgehog. He ran backwards and forwards for hours and didn't win once. How could he?

Mr. Hedgehog had been too clever for him, and in the end he had to part with one of his cabbages. He never did understand how it had happened. Mrs. Hedgehog said that really Mr. Hedgehog had cheated. But Mr. Hedgehog said, "Mr. Hare should not have made fun of my short legs. I wanted to teach him a lesson. Perhaps in future he will think twice before he is rude to someone."

Jack and the Beanstalk

Jack lived with his mother in a tumble down house. They were so poor they never seemed to have enough to eat, and one day, Jack's mother said,

"Jack, you must take the cow to market and sell her."

"If I do that we will have no milk," said Jack.

"If we don't sell her we will soon have nothing to eat at all," replied his mother.

And so, very sadly, Jack led the cow to market. He was about half way there when he met an old man.

"Is your cow for sale?" asked the old man. Jack said that she was.

"Then I'll give you five beans for her," said the old man. Jack laughed.

"You can't buy a cow with five beans," he said.

"Ah," said the old man, "But these are magic beans. You will make a fortune with them."

Jack couldn't resist such a good bargain. He gave the cow an affectionate pat, handed her halter to the old man, and took the five beans in exchange.

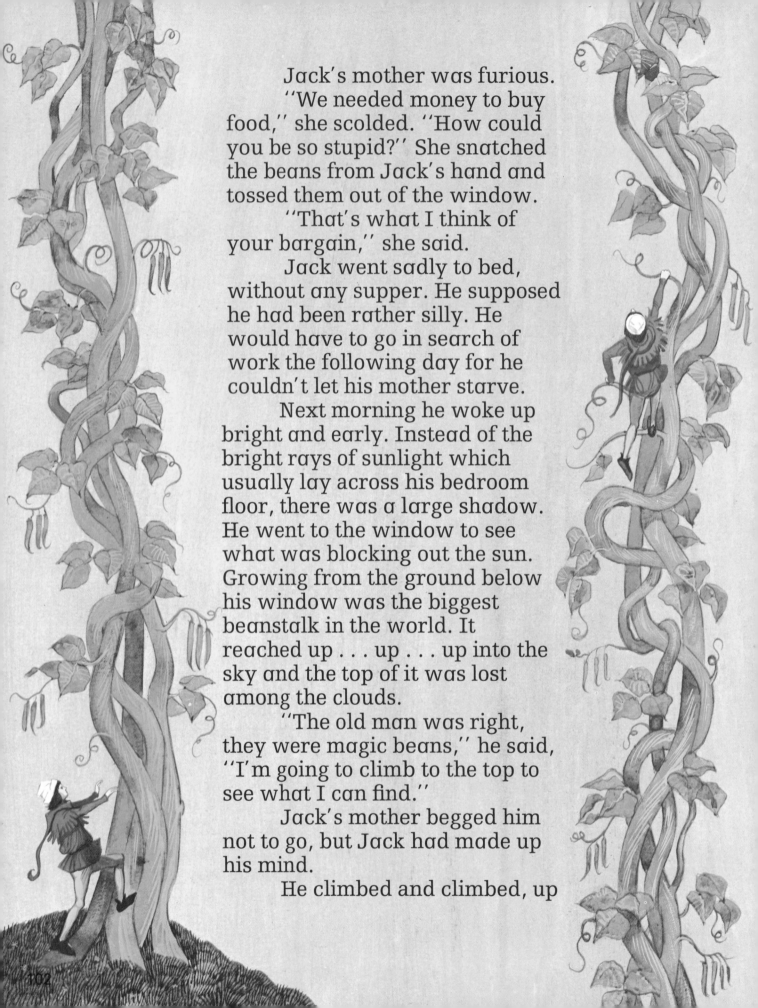

Jack's mother was furious. "We needed money to buy food," she scolded. "How could you be so stupid?" She snatched the beans from Jack's hand and tossed them out of the window.

"That's what I think of your bargain," she said.

Jack went sadly to bed, without any supper. He supposed he had been rather silly. He would have to go in search of work the following day for he couldn't let his mother starve.

Next morning he woke up bright and early. Instead of the bright rays of sunlight which usually lay across his bedroom floor, there was a large shadow. He went to the window to see what was blocking out the sun. Growing from the ground below his window was the biggest beanstalk in the world. It reached up . . . up . . . up into the sky and the top of it was lost among the clouds.

"The old man was right, they were magic beans," he said, "I'm going to climb to the top to see what I can find."

Jack's mother begged him not to go, but Jack had made up his mind.

He climbed and climbed, up

and up. He climbed through white swirling clouds until he came to the very tip of the beanstalk, and from the top of the beanstalk he stepped into another land. It was a land just like his own except that everything in it was twice and three times as big. All the climbing had made him hungry, so he went to the door of the only house he could see and knocked boldly. The door was opened by a huge woman. She was so big she was surely the wife of a giant. Jack persuaded her to give him some breakfast. He had just finished eating when he heard footsteps as heavy as falling boulders and then a voice as loud as thunder.

"FEE FI FO FUM, I SMELL THE BLOOD OF AN ENGLISHMAN!"

Quick as a flash, the giant woman bundled Jack into the oven.

"Sh . . . be very quiet," she said, "That's my husband. He eats boys like you for breakfast."

The huge woman, who was indeed the wife of a giant, told her husband he was mistaken and put a bowl of porridge on the table.

When he had eaten, the giant called for his hen.

"Lay!" he ordered. And the hen laid a golden egg.

Jack, who could see everything that was happening through a crack in the oven door, determined to have that hen for himself.

Presently the giant's head began to nod. Soon he was asleep. As quick as a bee about to sting, Jack left the oven, picked up the hen, ran to the top of the beanstalk and climbed down to earth again.

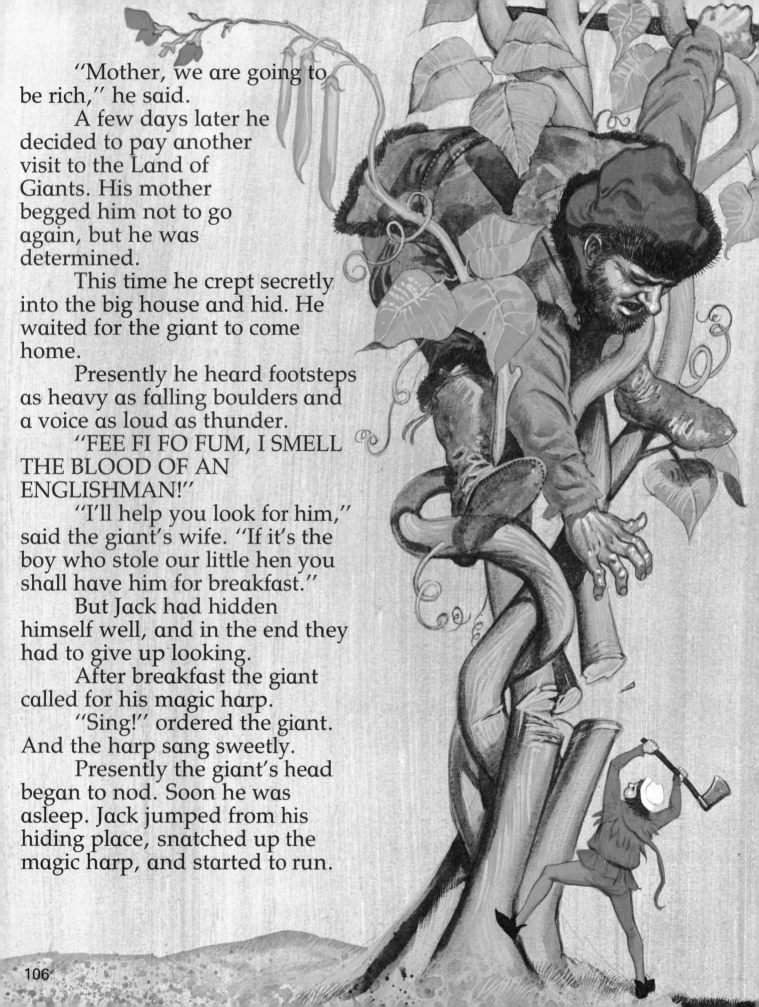

"Mother, we are going to be rich," he said.

A few days later he decided to pay another visit to the Land of Giants. His mother begged him not to go again, but he was determined.

This time he crept secretly into the big house and hid. He waited for the giant to come home.

Presently he heard footsteps as heavy as falling boulders and a voice as loud as thunder.

"FEE FI FO FUM, I SMELL THE BLOOD OF AN ENGLISHMAN!"

"I'll help you look for him," said the giant's wife. "If it's the boy who stole our little hen you shall have him for breakfast."

But Jack had hidden himself well, and in the end they had to give up looking.

After breakfast the giant called for his magic harp.

"Sing!" ordered the giant. And the harp sang sweetly.

Presently the giant's head began to nod. Soon he was asleep. Jack jumped from his hiding place, snatched up the magic harp, and started to run.

"Master! Master!" called the magic harp.

The giant woke with such a roar that the people in the land below the beanstalk thought the sky was falling in.

"FEE FI FO FUM. . ." he bellowed. "I *DO* SMELL THE BLOOD OF AN ENGLISHMAN. . ."

He ran after Jack with great lumbering, thundering steps. Jack was small and nimble, and had a good start. When he reached the top of the beanstalk he tucked the harp inside his shirt and began to climb down.

The beanstalk began to shake, and creak, and groan, as the angry giant followed him. . .

Faster went Jack . . . faster . . . and faster . . .

"Mother! . . ." he called as he neared the bottom. "Bring me an axe . . . quickly . . ."

He jumped to the ground and took the axe. He swung his arms as though he were the strongest man in the world, and with three hefty cuts the beanstalk came tumbling to the ground. There was a terrible roar as the giant fell. He made a hole so big, when he hit the ground, that both he and the beanstalk disappeared into it, and were lost forever.

As for Jack and his mother . . . well, they lived happily ever after with the hen who laid golden eggs, and the harp which sang beautiful songs. They were never poor again.

The Three Little Pigs

Once upon a time there were three little pigs who lived together in one house. As they grew bigger their house seemed to grow smaller, and one day they decided to build three separate houses.

The first little pig built himself a house of straw.

The second little pig built himself a house of sticks.

The third little pig built himself a house of bricks.

The house of bricks took much longer to build than the other two, but it was the strongest when it was finished.

Soon after the first little pig had moved into his house there was a knock at the door.

''Little pig, little pig let me come in,'' said the wily old wolf, thinking how nice it would be to have pig for dinner.

''No, no, by the hair of my chinny chin chin, I will not let you in,'' said the first little pig.

''Then I'll huff, and I'll puff, and I'll blow your house in,'' growled the wolf.

And that is exactly what he did. The straw house blew

away in the wind and the wolf gobbled up the pig.

When the wolf saw the house built of sticks, he licked his lips and said:

"Little pig, little pig, let me come in."

"No, no, by the hair of my chinny chin chin, I will not let you in," said the second little pig.

"Then I'll huff, and I'll puff, and I'll blow your house in," growled the wolf.

The house of sticks was as easy to blow down as the house of straw, and that was the end of the second little pig.

The wolf knew there was a third little pig about somewhere and when he saw the house of bricks he called through the letter box.

"Let me in little pig."

"No, no, by the hair of my chinny chin chin, I will not let you in," said the third little pig.

"Then I'll huff and I'll puff and I'll blow your house in," said the wolf.

And the wolf huffed and he

puffed, and he puffed and he huffed, until he was quite out of breath, and still the house of bricks stood firm and secure. It didn't even creak.

"I can see I'll have to be rather clever to catch this little pig," said the wolf. "I'll have to lure him outside his house."

He told the little pig about a field he knew where the turnips were ready for digging, and arranged to meet him there next morning.

But the third little pig was much cleverer than the wolf realised. He knew exactly what the wolf was up to. He had been to the field, dug up the turnips and was safely back indoors before the wolf had even woken up.

The wolf tried to keep his temper. He told the little pig about a tree he knew that was weighed down with juicy red apples.

"I'll meet you there in the morning," he said slyly.

The wolf wasn't going to be caught again and next day he

got up very early. When he reached the orchard the little pig was still in the tree picking apples.

"I'll throw you one," called the little pig, and he threw an apple so that it rolled into the long grass.

While the wolf was looking for it the little pig jumped from the tree and ran home. He was safely inside his brick house before the wolf realised he had been tricked.

By this time the wolf was getting very annoyed . . .

and hungry.

"I'll meet you at the fair tomorrow," he said.

The little pig did go to the fair next day. He bought himself a butter churn. He was on his way home when he caught sight of the wolf. As quick as a raindrop hiding in a puddle, he hid himself in the butter churn and began to roll down the hill. He rolled right over the wolf's foot and frightened him horribly. He was safely inside his brick house before the wolf stopped trembling.

When the wolf discovered who had been inside the butter churn he was very angry indeed. He was determined that the little pig should not escape again. He climbed on to the roof of the brick house and began to ease himself down the brick chimney.

The little pig was very frightened when he heard the wolf mumbling and grumbling inside his chimney, but he didn't panic. He built up the fire and set his biggest cooking pot on the flames.

The wolf slithered down the chimney and fell into the pot with an enormous splash and a very loud OUCH!!! And that, I am glad to say, was the end of the wolf.

SNOW-WHITE AND ROSE-RED

Once there was a woman who lived in a lonely cottage in the middle of a wood. She had two daughters, one called Snow-White, and the other Rose-Red. One winter evening, when they were all sitting by the fire, there was a knock at the door.

"Someone must be seeking shelter from the cold," said the woman and went to open the door.

Standing on the doorstep, his black fur sprinkled with snow, was an enormous bear. Snow-White and Rose-Red took one look at his bright shining eyes, and his powerful claws, and ran to hide.

"You look very cold," said the woman to the bear. "Please come in and warm yourself by the fire."

"Do not be afraid," said the bear when he saw the children peeping at him. "I will not harm you."

"Will you help me brush the snow from my fur?" asked the bear, as the children crept nervously from their hiding place. They picked up the broom so that they could brush him without getting too close, but the bear was so friendly and it was such fun brushing a bear with a broom they soon forgot to be afraid.

The bear came to the house and slept by the fire every night throughout the long winter. He and the children became firm friends, and no matter how roughly the children played, the bear was always very gentle.

Then one day, as summer grew near, the bear said goodbye.

"I must go and protect my treasure from the dwarfs," he said. "They stay underground in winter but in summer they get everywhere. I fear they are not to be trusted."

One day, later that summer, when Snow-White and Rose-Red were in the wood picking wild strawberries, they saw a dwarf themselves. He was jumping up and down in a terrible rage. The end of his beard had caught in a crack in a fallen log and he couldn't get it out.

"How did it happen?" asked Snow-White, as she and Rose-Red did their best to pull him free.

"Not that it's any business of yours," grumbled the dwarf, "but I was driving a wedge into the crack to keep it open. The wedge popped out and the crack closed up again over my beard . . . Ouch! Ouch! You're hurting me! Be careful!"

"We can't get you out on our own," said Rose-Red. "I'll go and get some help."

"I can't wait that long . . . think of something yourself," grumpled the dwarf. And so Snow-White, thinking the dwarf would be pleased, took the scissors, which she always carried in her pocket, and cut through his beard. He was free, but the tip of his beard was growing out of the log like a fuzzy white fungus. The dwarf wasn't at all pleased. He picked up the sack of gold which was lying beside the log, and stomped off, without even the hint of a thank you.

A few days later, Snow-White and Rose-Red went to the river to catch fish. Who should they see there but the very same dwarf. He was in terrible trouble. The end of his beard had caught in his fishing line, and a fish was pulling the line, and him, into the river.

"Help me! Help me!" shrieked the dwarf, holding as tightly as he could to a bunch of reeds. He was slipping all the time.

"We must do something quickly or he will drown," said Rose-Red.

Snow-White took out her scissors and snipped the end off the dwarf's beard. The dwarf fell backwards into the reeds and the fish swam away. Was the dwarf grateful? Not at all! He picked up a sack of pearls which was lying in the reeds and stomped off with a bad-tempered glare and not even a hint of a thank you.

Some time later, Snow-White and Rose-Red were crossing the heath when an eagle, which had been hovering over a rock, suddenly swooped low. There was a terrible cry. They ran to see what had happened. The eagle had its talons in the dwarf's coat and was lifting him from the ground.

"Help me!" shrieked the dwarf. Snow-White and Rose-Red caught hold of his legs and pulled . . . downwards. The eagle held on tight with his talons and pulled . . . upwards.

"You'll tear me in two!" shrieked the dwarf. But all that was torn was his coat, as the eagle continued to soar upwards and HE fell with a thud to the ground. Was he grateful at being rescued? No, he wasn't. "You should have been more careful, then you wouldn't have torn my coat," he grumbled. He picked up a sack of precious stones which was lying beside the rock and disappeared into a cave. Snow-White and Rose-Red were quite used to the dwarf's grumpy ways by now. They didn't expect a thank you. Which was just as well, because they didn't get one.

Later in the afternoon they caught the dwarf by surprise. He had emptied the sack of precious stones onto the ground and was gloating over their colours and their sparkle. He stamped his feet and shook his fists when he saw them. He was VERY annoyed.

"How DARE you spy on me!" he shouted. In the very middle of his rage an enormous black bear came ambling along the path.

36

The dwarf turned as pale as an uncooked pancake, and ran towards his cave. But the bear was quicker than he was and stood in his way.

"Don't eat me . . . please don't eat me!" The dwarf was shivering with fright. "You can have ALL my treasure! I'm too small and thin to eat! Eat those two wicked girls!"

The bear raised his paw and knocked the dwarf to the ground. Snow-White and Rose-Red were very frightened, but the bear called to them not to be afraid and they recognised his voice. As they ran to him, his bearskin fell to the ground. He wasn't a bear at all, but a king who had been bewitched by the dwarf, and the treasure the dwarf had been gloating over was his. Now the bad-tempered dwarf was dead, and the spell was broken.

Puss in Boots

Once upon a time, there was a miller, who had three sons. When he died he left his mill to his first son, his donkey to his second son, and because he had nothing else, he left his cat to his third son.

The first son ground flour at the mill and sold it. The second son harnessed the donkey to a cart and carried things for paying customers. But what could the third son do with a cat, except let him sit in the sun, and purr, and drink milk?

One day, the cat said, "Master, give me a pair of boots and a sack and you will see that I am not as useless as you think." It was a very strange request for a cat to make, but it was granted nonetheless.

The cat, or Puss in Boots, as the miller's son now called him, went into the forest and caught a rabbit. He put it in the sack and then instead of taking it home to the miller's son, he took it to the King's palace.

"Please accept this small present from my master the Marquis of Carabas," said Puss in Boots.

It was to be the first of many presents Puss in Boots took to the King, and each time he said he had been sent by his master the Marquis of Carabas. And though the King never actually met the Marquis of Carabas, he soon became very familiar with his name. The miller's son knew nothing of the presents, or of the Marquis of Carabas, and Puss in Boots didn't tell him.

One day, when Puss in Boots was at the palace, he overheard someone say that the King was about to take his daughter for a drive in the country. Puss in Boots hurried home.

"Quick master!" he called. "Go and bathe in the river and I will make your fortune."

It was another strange request for a cat to make but the miller's son was used to his pet by now and so he did as he was told. No sooner was he in the river than Puss in Boots took his clothes and threw them into the river with him.

"Puss . . . Puss . . . what are you doing?" called the miller's son.

Puss didn't answer, he was watching the road. Presently he saw the King's carriage in the distance. He waited until it was close then he ran out in the road in front of it.

"Help! Help! My master the Marquis of Carabas is drowning! Please save him!"

It took but a moment to drag the miller's son, who hadn't the slightest idea what Puss in Boots was up to, from the river and find him some dry clothes. He looked so handsome in the fine velvet tunic and the doublet and hose borrowed from one of the footmen that the princess fell in love with him at once.

"Father dear, may the Marquis of Carabas ride with us?"

The King liked to please his daughter and agreed to her request at once.

"Will you ride with us Puss?" asked the King.

Puss asked to be excused. He said he had something rather important to attend to. He ran on ahead of the carriage, and each time he saw someone at work in the fields he called,

"If the King asks who this land belongs to, tell him it belongs to the Marquis of Carabas."

The King did stop the carriage several times, and each time he received the same answer to his question.

'The Marquis of Carabas must be a very rich man,' he thought.

Puss in Boots ran so swiftly that soon he was a long way ahead of the carriage. Presently he came to a rich and imposing looking castle, which he knew belonged to a cruel and wicked ogre. He went straight up to the ogre without so much as a twitching of a whisker, and said,

"I hear you can turn yourself into any animal you choose. I won't believe a story like that unless I see it for myself."

Immediately, the ogre changed himself into a lion, and roared and growled and snarled.

"There . . ." he said, when he had turned himself back into an ogre. "I hope I frightened you."

"Must be easy to change your-self into something big," said Puss in Boots with a shrug. "I don't suppose you can turn your-self into something as small as a . . . er . . . um . . ." He seemed to be thinking. ". . . er . . . um . . . a mouse?"

The ogre couldn't have a mere cat doubting his special abilities. He changed himself into a tiny mouse in the twinkling of an eye. It was the last time he changed himself into anything because Puss in Boots pounced on him and ate him up before he could change back into an ogre, and THAT was the end of him!

"Hoorah!" shouted the castle servants. "We are free of the wicked ogre at last. Hoorah!"

"Your new master will always be kind, you can be sure of that," said Puss in Boots.

"Who IS our new master?" they asked.

"The Marquis of Carabas of course," said Puss.

When the King's carriage reached the castle, Puss in Boots was standing at the drawbridge, with the smiling servants gathered round him.

"Welcome . ." he said with a beautiful bow. "Welcome to the home of my master the Marquis of Carabas." The miller's son was too astonished to do anything except think to himself,

'Whatever is Puss up to?'

Luckily Puss had time to explain while the King was getting out of the carriage.

'What a rich man this Marquis must be,' thought the King. 'And such a nice young man too.'

Not long afterwards the princess and the miller's son were married. They, and Puss in Boots, lived happily ever after in the castle that had once belonged to the wicked ogre.

PEAS

A gardener kneeling on his knees
Planted several rows of peas.
The sunshine shone, the breezes blew,
And all the little peapods grew.

Then, in the night, from a nearby hole,
A family of mice to the garden stole.
They climbed the stems with the greatest ease,
And that was the end of the garden of peas!

BIG BALL

The big ball bounced from off the floor,
The big ball bounced straight out of the door;
The big ball bounced through the garden gate,
The big ball bounced along the street.
Farther and farther, up and down,
The big ball bounced right through the town;
It bounced along the country lanes,
It bounced through several window panes.
Along the river, up the hill,
Through the meadow, by the mill;
Higher and higher it bounced, and soon
It landed on the rising moon.

Pip The Pup

Pip the Pup trotted out into the garden and sniffed the sweet morning air. He was feeling ready for anything. He looked this way and that way and behind him. And then he saw his tail. It stopped wagging as soon as he looked at it.

He looked at it with one eye for a time. He couldn't make up his mind whether it belonged to him or whether it was something that followed him about.

Pip was only a baby puppy, and there were lots of things he wasn't sure about. The tail was one of them.

The tail didn't move or make a sound. Pip gave a sharp bark at it to warn it that he had got his eye on it and it must not try any tricks on him.

Then he went on his way, growling loudly to show anybody who happened to be about that he was a dangerous fellow.

A sparrow hopped on to the lawn. Pip made a dash at it, but tripped and fell nose-first into a flower-bed. The sparrow went on hopping around just as if Pip wasn't there, so Pip barked furiously to show he wasn't a dog to be ignored.

Then he stopped and listened. Somebody was barking back! "Wuff, wuff, wuff!" barked Pip sharply. Then he cocked his head on one side and listened. "Wuff, wuff, wuff!"

He was right! Someone was answering him. Another dog! Off down the garden path dashed Pip, through the gate and into the lane. He just fancied a jolly romp with a dog friend. But which was the way to take?

Pip hesitated, not certain whether to go up or down the lane or over the meadow. Then he saw Harry the Horse trotting towards him down the lane.

"Excuse me," he said politely, "but do you know where another dog lives around here?"

"There are no dogs round here," snorted Harry. "You're the only dog, and you're not really a dog—yet. Good day!"

Harry splashed through a puddle in the lane and went on his way. Pip went thoughtfully over to the puddle and had a drink. Then he sat down in it and had a think.

Just then, Mrs. Penny Pig came bustling down the lane, followed by all her eight piglets, in single file.

"Oh, good morning, Mrs. Pig," said Pip. "Please can you tell me where another dog lives round here?"

"ANOTHER dog?" Mrs. Pig grunted. "What do you mean, ANOTHER dog? There aren't any dogs round here, and I hope there never will be."

"But I suppose," she added, looking sharply at Pip with her beady eyes, "I suppose YOU will be a dog some day. Come along, piglets, or we shall be late for market."

She hurried off, with her eight piglets squealing to each other behind her.

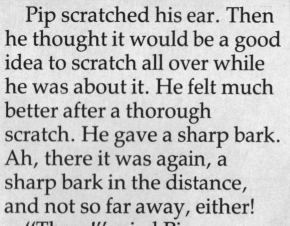

Pip scratched his ear. Then he thought it would be a good idea to scratch all over while he was about it. He felt much better after a thorough scratch. He gave a sharp bark. Ah, there it was again, a sharp bark in the distance, and not so far away, either!

"There!" cried Pip delightedly. "I wasn't mistaken. Wuff, wuff, wuff!"

"Wuff, wuff, wuff!" came the answering bark again.

Happily, Pip ran off up the lane, giving a sharp bark every now and again to let the other dog know he was coming. And the other dog barked back! At any moment now he would run into the other dog, thought Pip. He was so excited that he didn't really look where he was going, and instead of running into the other dog he ran right into a wall. It was a high wall and a hard wall. Pip backed away. He sat down and rubbed his nose with his paw. He looked up at the wall and barked at it thoughtfully. The other dog barked back, very loudly, just in front of him!

"Why," cried Pip, "the other dog's there, just on the other side of the wall. Wuff, wuff, wuff!"

At that moment, there was a rustling and a stirring high up in a tree close by. The enormous eyes of Mrs. Owl peered down at Pip. "Whatever is the meaning of this dreadful noise?" she scolded. "Don't you know I go to sleep during the day? How dare you make such a disturbance!"

"Oh, dear!" said Pip, "I'm very sorry, Mrs. Owl. I forgot you would be in bed. I was just saying hello to the other dog behind the wall."

"Other dog? What other dog?" said Mrs. Owl. "There's no dog behind the wall, or in front of it, either," she added, peering down at the baby puppy, "because YOU can hardly be called a dog."

"There is a dog," said Pip. "Listen! You can hear him bark at me. Wuff, wuff, wuff!"

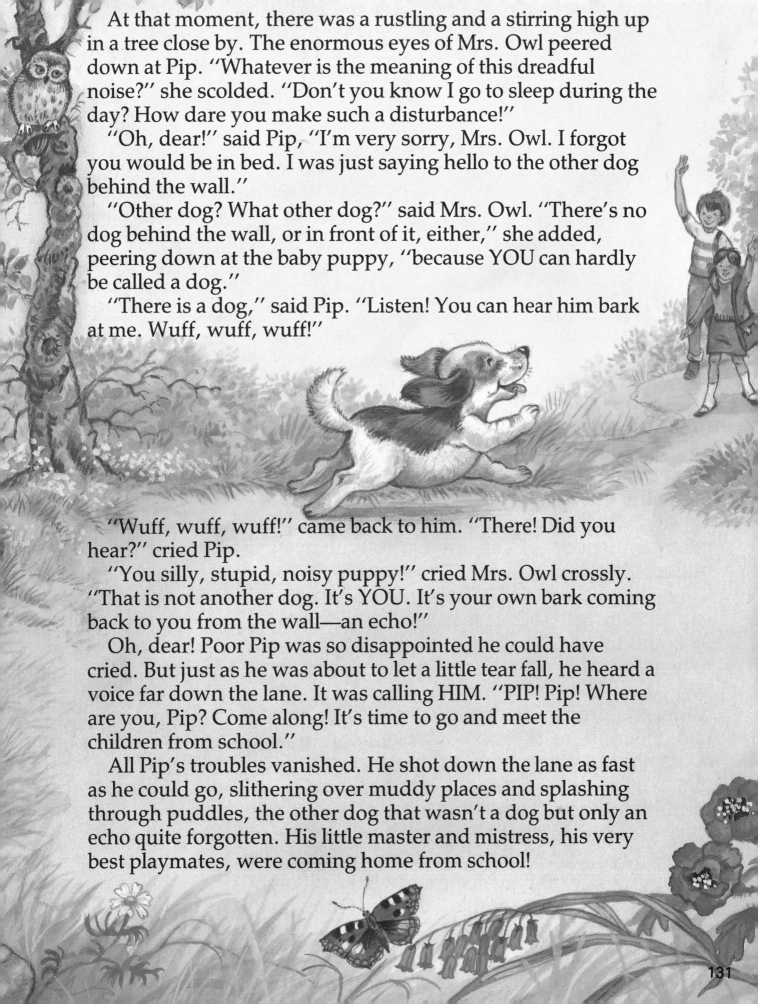

"Wuff, wuff, wuff!" came back to him. "There! Did you hear?" cried Pip.

"You silly, stupid, noisy puppy!" cried Mrs. Owl crossly. "That is not another dog. It's YOU. It's your own bark coming back to you from the wall—an echo!"

Oh, dear! Poor Pip was so disappointed he could have cried. But just as he was about to let a little tear fall, he heard a voice far down the lane. It was calling HIM. "PIP! Pip! Where are you, Pip? Come along! It's time to go and meet the children from school."

All Pip's troubles vanished. He shot down the lane as fast as he could go, slithering over muddy places and splashing through puddles, the other dog that wasn't a dog but only an echo quite forgotten. His little master and mistress, his very best playmates, were coming home from school!

The Princess

Once there was a prince who wanted to marry a Princess. He travelled far and wide, for many months, searching for one. He met many girls who said they were Princesses, but somehow he could never be quite sure they were telling him the truth.

It was a very sad Prince who returned alone to the palace.

One dark night, not long after his return, there was a dreadful storm. It rained, and it thundered, and bright flashes of lightning lit up the sky. Everyone was saying how glad he was not to be outside, when there was a knock at the palace door. The King himself went to answer it.

A wet bedraggled girl stood shivering on the doorstep. "Come in, come in at once," he cried, "You must shelter here for the night."

When the girl was dry and warm again, and had eaten supper, she told them that she was a Princess. The Prince wished he could believe her, for of all the girls who said they were Princesses, this was the one he most wanted to believe.

Now the Prince's mother was very wise, and that night, without telling anyone what she was doing she re-made the girl's bed. She put one tiny pea on the smooth wooden bed . . . and on top of the pea she put twenty soft mattresses . . . and on top of the mattresses, she put twenty, very soft, feather pillows. The girl had to climb almost to the ceiling before she could get into it!

Next morning the Queen asked her how well she had slept.

"I hardly slept at all," sighed the girl. "The bed was so lumpy, I tossed and turned and twisted all night."

As soon as she heard that, the Queen took the girl by the hand and led her to the Prince.

and the Pea

"Only a real Princess could lie on so many soft mattresses and be unable to sleep because of one tiny pea," she said. And she explained to everyone what she had done.

The Prince was overjoyed, and he and the Princess were married, and of course they lived happily ever after. Princes and Princesses always do.

Hidden Magic

One morning, when the mist was lying over the hills and the air was crisp and chilly, John the Ploughman took his plough from the barn and walked to a field that was overgrown with grass and tall weeds.

He enjoyed ploughing. He liked watching as the plough turned the earth and cut brown furrows that were as straight and true as lines ruled on paper with a ruler.

As the sun rose higher in the sky the mist cleared. It was going to be a fine day. John the Ploughman whistled along with the birds and was happy in his work.

He had reached the halfway mark and was turning his plough, when he thought he heard a strange sound. His ears were used to outdoor noises. Anything, even slightly unusual, caught his attention at once. He stood still and listened intently. The birds were singing in the hedgerow, the mice were scurrying in the undergrowth, the breeze was whispering in the leaves . . . but there WAS something else. It was very faint . . . but there it was again.

"I can hear someone crying," he said to a blackbird sitting on a branch.

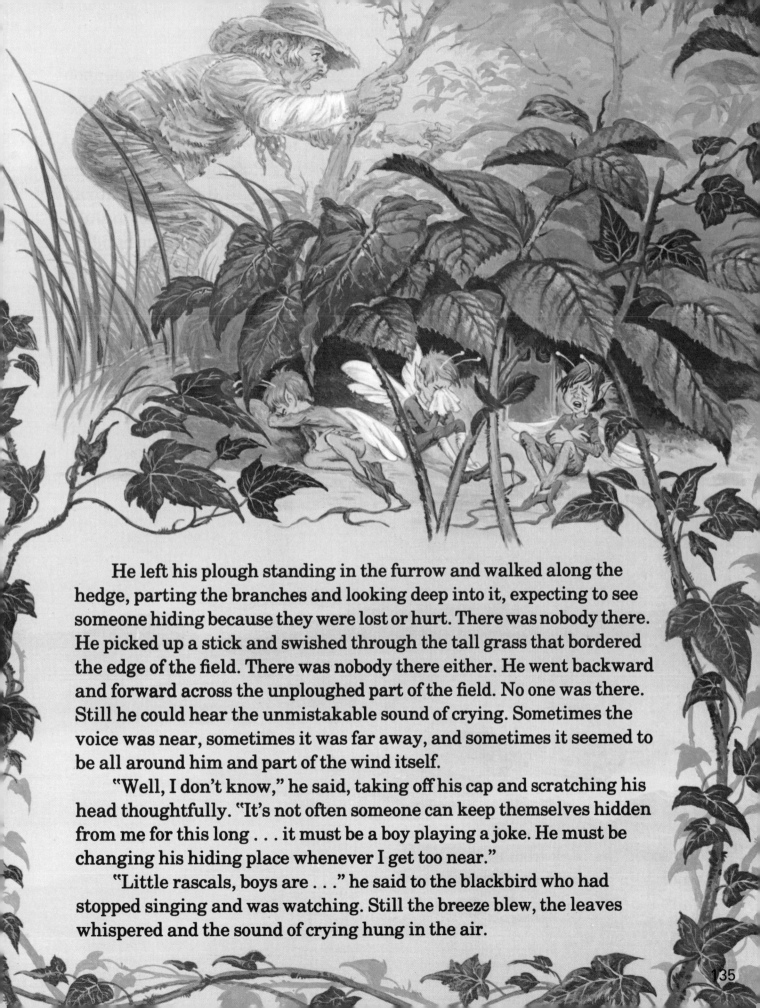

He left his plough standing in the furrow and walked along the hedge, parting the branches and looking deep into it, expecting to see someone hiding because they were lost or hurt. There was nobody there. He picked up a stick and swished through the tall grass that bordered the edge of the field. There was nobody there either. He went backward and forward across the unploughed part of the field. No one was there. Still he could hear the unmistakable sound of crying. Sometimes the voice was near, sometimes it was far away, and sometimes it seemed to be all around him and part of the wind itself.

"Well, I don't know," he said, taking off his cap and scratching his head thoughtfully. "It's not often someone can keep themselves hidden from me for this long . . . it must be a boy playing a joke. He must be changing his hiding place whenever I get too near."

"Little rascals, boys are . . ." he said to the blackbird who had stopped singing and was watching. Still the breeze blew, the leaves whispered and the sound of crying hung in the air.

John the Ploughman was about to admit that he had been beaten in a game of hide-and-seek by a boy, when he saw something lying on a flat stone close by the bottom of the hedge. It was a tiny shovel with a long handle. Picking it up carefully, John saw at once that the handle had been broken making it impossible to use.

"Ah, now I understand," said John softly. "The boy who is crying and hiding at the same time isn't playing a joke after all . . . he wants me to mend his shovel and is too shy to ask . . . boys are funny."

John cut a straight twig from the hedge with his pocket knife and stripped the bark from it. It only took him a few minutes to make it into a new handle for the shovel.

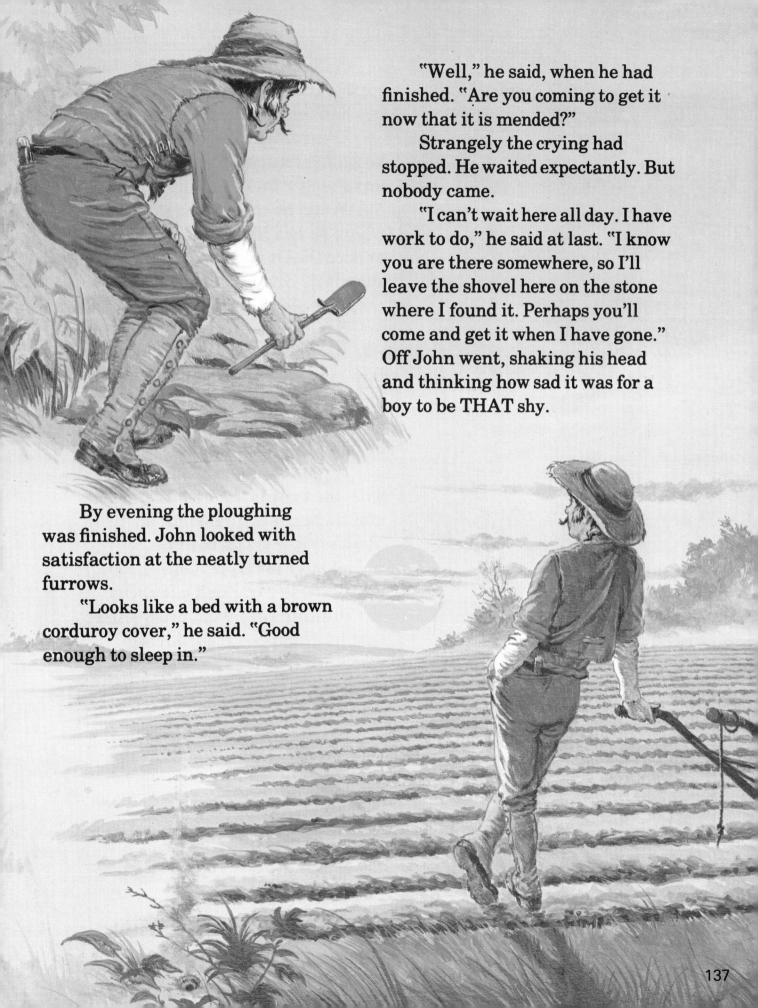

"Well," he said, when he had finished. "Are you coming to get it now that it is mended?"

Strangely the crying had stopped. He waited expectantly. But nobody came.

"I can't wait here all day. I have work to do," he said at last. "I know you are there somewhere, so I'll leave the shovel here on the stone where I found it. Perhaps you'll come and get it when I have gone." Off John went, shaking his head and thinking how sad it was for a boy to be THAT shy.

By evening the ploughing was finished. John looked with satisfaction at the neatly turned furrows.

"Looks like a bed with a brown corduroy cover," he said. "Good enough to sleep in."

As John walked home along the edge of the field he wondered if the boy had come back for his shovel.

"I'll go round by the hedgerow," he said. "It won't take any longer and then I'll know for sure."

When he came to the stone where he had laid the shovel he saw at once that it had gone. To his surprise, lying in the same place on the same stone, was a tiny loaf of bread.

It smelled so delicious that he couldn't resist popping it into his mouth. He could not remember ever tasting anything so marvellous before.

As John walked home, still with the taste of the bread in his mouth, he thought to himself, 'Perhaps it wasn't a boy I heard crying after all . . . perhaps . . . but no, of course it couldn't have been . . .'

But thinking about everything that had happened that day, he wondered all the same.

As well he might, for the field he had ploughed that day lay like a roof over a fairy village. The shovel he had found was used every day by the fairy baker to lift the hot bread, pies and beautiful cakes as light as thistledown out of the oven. Once the shovel was broken everyone went hungry and the crying of the children was what John had heard.

Now all was well. The children were happy and the baker was hard at work again. John still wondered about the little shovel with a long handle and the little loaf he found every Spring when he came to plough the field once more.

The Tale Of The Turnip

One day, Grandpa Brown planted a turnip seed in a corner of his vegetable patch. He watered it, and pulled the weeds from around it, and it grew bigger and bigger and BIGGER.

When it was as big round, as his wife's tape measure was long, and that was very big round indeed, Grandpa Brown said, "Wife, I fancy turnip broth for my dinner today, I will pull the turnip. When it is cooked we will have a feast fit for a king." He went to the vegetable patch and took hold of the turnip's green leaves, which by now reached almost as high as his chin, and pulled. And then he pulled a bit harder. Nothing happened. The turnip was stuck tight in the ground.

"Wife!" he called. "Please come and help me."

"Why are you taking so long?" asked Grandma Brown.

"Do not waste your breath talking wife, just put your arms round my waist, and when I say pull, pull."

"Yes husband," said Grandma Brown.

"Pull!" said Grandpa Brown. Grandpa Brown AND Grandma Brown pulled and pulled. Still the turnip did not move.

"Grandson!" called Grandma Brown. "Please come and help us."

"Fancy not being strong enough to pull a turnip from the ground," said the boy trying not to laugh.

"Do not waste breath laughing," said Grandma Brown. "Put your arms round my waist and when Grandpa says pull, pull."

"Pull!" said Grandpa Brown. Grandpa Brown, Grandma Brown AND the boy pulled and pulled. Still the turnip would not move.

"Sister!" called the boy. "Please come and help us."

"I am hungry, when will the broth be ready?" asked the girl.

"Do not waste breath talking," said the boy. "Put your arms round my waist and when Grandpa says pull, pull."

"Pull!" said Grandpa Brown. Grandpa Brown, Grandma Brown, the boy AND the girl pulled and pulled. It really was a very stubborn turnip.

"Dog!" called the girl. "Please come and help us."

"Woof!" said the dog.

"Do not waste breath barking," said the girl. "When Grandpa says pull, pull."

"Pull!" said Grandpa Brown. Grandpa Brown, Grandma Brown, the boy, the girl AND the dog pulled and pulled and PULLED. But it was all wasted effort. The turnip stuck in the ground as fast as glue sticks in a gluepot.

"Cat!" called the dog. "Please come and help us."

"Miaow!" said the cat.

"Do not waste breath miaowing," said the dog. "When Grandpa says pull, pull."

"Pull!" said Grandpa Brown. Grandpa Brown, Grandma Brown, the boy, the girl, the dog AND the cat pulled as hard as they possibly could. The turnip roots pulled even harder.

It really was the stubbornest turnip any of them had ever seen.

"We might as well give up," said Grandpa Brown sadly. "We cannot pull the turnip and we will never have our turnip broth."

"What a pity," sighed Grandma Brown. "I was quite looking forward to making it."

"And I was looking forward to eating it," sighed the boy, the girl, the dog and the cat, one after the other.

"Let me help," squeaked a voice at their feet. It was a mouse who had come from his hole to see what all the sighing was about.

Grandpa Brown shook his head sadly. "The tiny amount of help you can give will make no difference at all," he said.

"At least let him try," said Grandma Brown, the boy, the girl, the dog and the cat, all at the same time.

And so once again Grandpa Brown said, "Pull!" and once again Grandpa Brown, Grandma Brown, the boy, the girl, the dog, the cat, and this time the mouse as well, pulled . . . and PULLED.

And then, so suddenly that they were all taken by surprise, the turnip came up from the ground in a shower of soil and tiny pebbles and they all fell backwards one on top of the other, with the turnip on top of them all.

When the broth was finally made, there was a special helping in a special dish for the mouse, for without his help there would have been no turnip broth at all.

WIZARD BEANIE

In those far off days in 'once upon a time' land there lived a good kind wizard. He was called Wizard Beanie because he was so tall and thin that he looked like a bean pole.

Now the house where he lived was almost a ruin and everyone told him he should do something about it. But Wizard Beanie never seemed to have the time.

"Why don't you magic yourself a new house?" someone asked him.

"What a good idea, I never thought of it," said the wizard.

He looked up all his old spells but the only one he could find was for making a palace and that would be much too big for him. So he set to work to make his own spell. Then he put on his hat, nodded his head three times, waved his wand and hey presto, the ruin disappeared and a house stood there instead.

But there was one thing wrong with it. The house wasn't high enough for Wizard Beanie. He was bent almost double and could not stand up at all. Thinking he had made a mistake, he did the spell again but the same thing happened.

He crawled out of the door and straightened himself. He could see over the roof top easily.

Wizard Beanie scratched his head. Now what was he to do? It looked a good strong house. It would be warm and dry in the winter, but it was no use to him as he would be most uncomfortable bent double all day.

Then he had an idea and chuckling to himself, he crawled back in and worked another spell.

At once the spell began to work; he could feel himself shrinking and in no time at all he could stand up quite comfortably in his new home. But now instead of being like a bean pole he was short and fat. Yes, – fat! That was something he wasn't expecting but luckily his clothes stretched so he did not burst out of them. One other thing had gone wrong too, but he did not know about that yet.

Some of the people from the village had noticed the new house and had come to look at it.

"Not very high, is it?" said one.

"How on earth is Wizard Beanie going to stand up in there?" asked another.

Wizard Beanie smiled to himself and went out to greet them.

Everyone stared at him in amazement.

"Hello," he greeted them.

"Who are you?" one of them asked.

"Who am I? Wizard Beanie, of course," he answered looking surprised.

A crowd had gathered by now and they started muttering.

"What have you done with our wizard?" one shouted.

"Yes," threatened the crowd. "What have you done with him?"

"But I *am* Beanie," protested the puzzled wizard. "I have only made myself smaller to fit my new house."

"Wizard Beanie had black hair, yours is red," called out a little boy.

"Red? Good heavens!" gasped Beanie. "Are you sure?"

"Of course we are sure," retorted an old dame. "Look." She handed him

146 a small mirror.

"Thank you Mary," said the Wizard. "How is your rheumatism today?"

Then he looked into the mirror and he had such a shock. His hair was indeed red and he did not look like himself at all.

"Oh well," he admitted. "I suppose I cannot blame you for being suspicious when I look like this."

"Well John," he said looking at the man next to him. "Is Daisy the cow better today? And you, Frank. How is your wife now? Feeling alright again?"

The people gazed at him. How did he know them all if he wasn't Wizard Beanie? Then he started to laugh and he was so fat he shook like a jelly.

"The trouble is," he chuckled. "My spells never seem to work for myself. Anyway, I must do something to look like my old self again."

He went back into the new house and when he came out the crowd gasped. His hair was black again and he wasn't half as fat.

"Ah, that feels better," he sighed. "Do I look more like myself now?"

Everybody laughed and cheered. They gathered around him to touch him or clap him on the back.

"You are still plump," said Mary. "Or perhaps I should say portly."

"We can't call you Beanie anymore," said Frank.

"I think I would rather be portly than look like a bean pole," smiled the wizard.

"We will call you Wizard Portly then," laughed John.

"Hip-hip-hurray for Wizard Portly," shouted the children.

Everyone cheered loudly and they were all happy again in 'once upon a time' land.

A Tug-O-War

All was peaceful in the forest. The birds were singing, animals were grazing, butterflies were flitting, Mother Sparrow was sitting on her nest waiting for Father Sparrow to bring her a worm. Father Sparrow was at the waterhole.

"Move over Mr. Crocodile," he said. "I want to drink."

Mr. Crocodile opened one lazy eye. "If I want to lay in the waterhole, then I will," he said. "Go and find a drink somewhere else."

Father Sparrow was cross, but how can a sparrow argue with a crocodile?

He found a worm and took it to Mother Sparrow. He was sitting in the tree beside her when there was a tremendous bump. The tree shook and trembled as though it was about to fall.

"What's happening?" chirped Mother Sparrow anxiously. If the tree fell, their nest would fall too and her eggs would break.

"It's Mr. Elephant," said Father Sparrow. "Hey there Mr. Elephant, why don't you look where you are going? You nearly shook our nest from the tree."

Mr. Elephant said nothing.

"You might say you are sorry," said Father Sparrow.

"I might, but I'm not going to," said Mr. Elephant.

Father Sparrow was very annoyed at his rudeness. "I'll tie you up if you dare to do it again," he said.

Mr. Elephant laughed. "YOU tie ME up, ha . . . ha . . ." and he plodded off into the forest rumbling and gurgling with laughter.

"Just you wait and see," said Father Sparrow. He flew down to the waterhole. Mr. Crocodile was still bathing and he still would not let anyone near enough to get a drink. "If you don't come out of there I'll tie you up," said Father Sparrow.

"You might tie me, but you'll never hold me," laughed Mr. Crocodile.

"We shall see," said Father Sparrow and went in search of an extra long, extra strong vine.

The next time Mr. Elephant passed by the tree in which the sparrows had their nest, he bumped into it deliberately.

"Oh . . . oh . . ." cheeped Mother Sparrow.

"I'm going to tie you up," said Father Sparrow sternly.

"You might tie me, but you'll never hold me," laughed Mr. Elephant. And just to show that he wasn't afraid, he stood still and let Father Sparrow fly over his back and under his tummy with the vine and tie it in a knot.

151

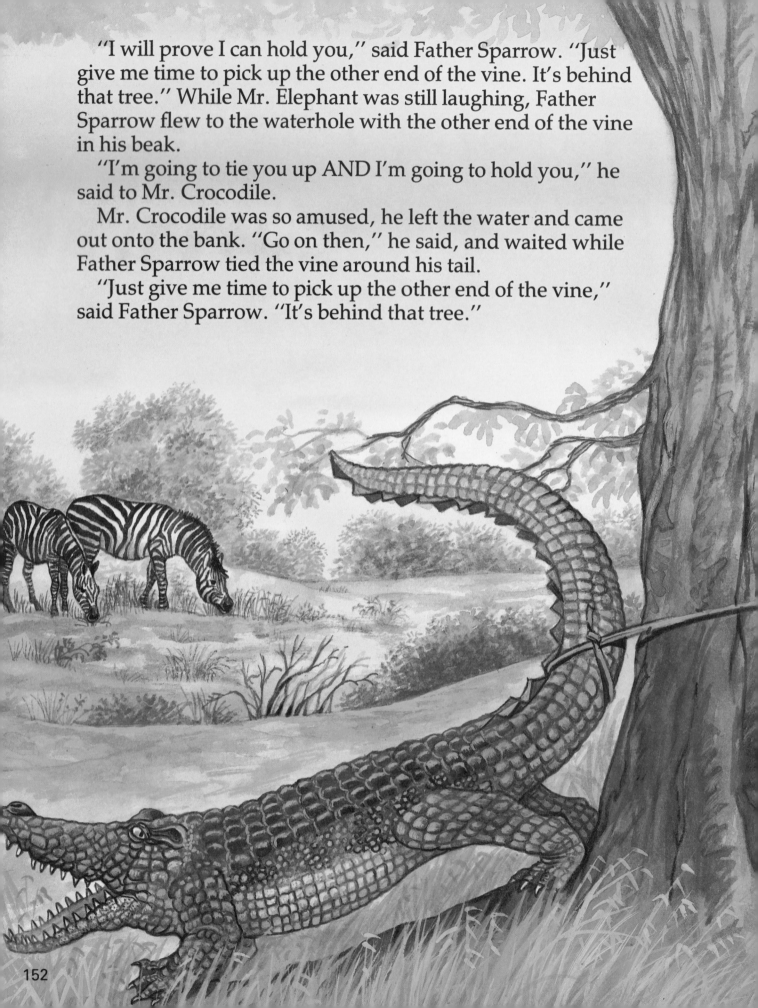

"I will prove I can hold you," said Father Sparrow. "Just give me time to pick up the other end of the vine. It's behind that tree." While Mr. Elephant was still laughing, Father Sparrow flew to the waterhole with the other end of the vine in his beak.

"I'm going to tie you up AND I'm going to hold you," he said to Mr. Crocodile.

Mr. Crocodile was so amused, he left the water and came out onto the bank. "Go on then," he said, and waited while Father Sparrow tied the vine around his tail.

"Just give me time to pick up the other end of the vine," said Father Sparrow. "It's behind that tree."

Father Sparrow hid in the trees, and then called loudly, "Start pulling . . . NOW!"

Mr. Elephant began to pull. Mr. Crocodile began to pull. They both thought they were pulling Father Sparrow. Instead they were pulling each other. How they grunted and puffed!

"That sparrow is incredibly strong," grunted Mr. Elephant.

"That sparrow must be the strongest bird in the world," puffed Mr. Crocodile.

Mr. Crocodile and Mr. Elephant were very well matched. Neither one could move the other.

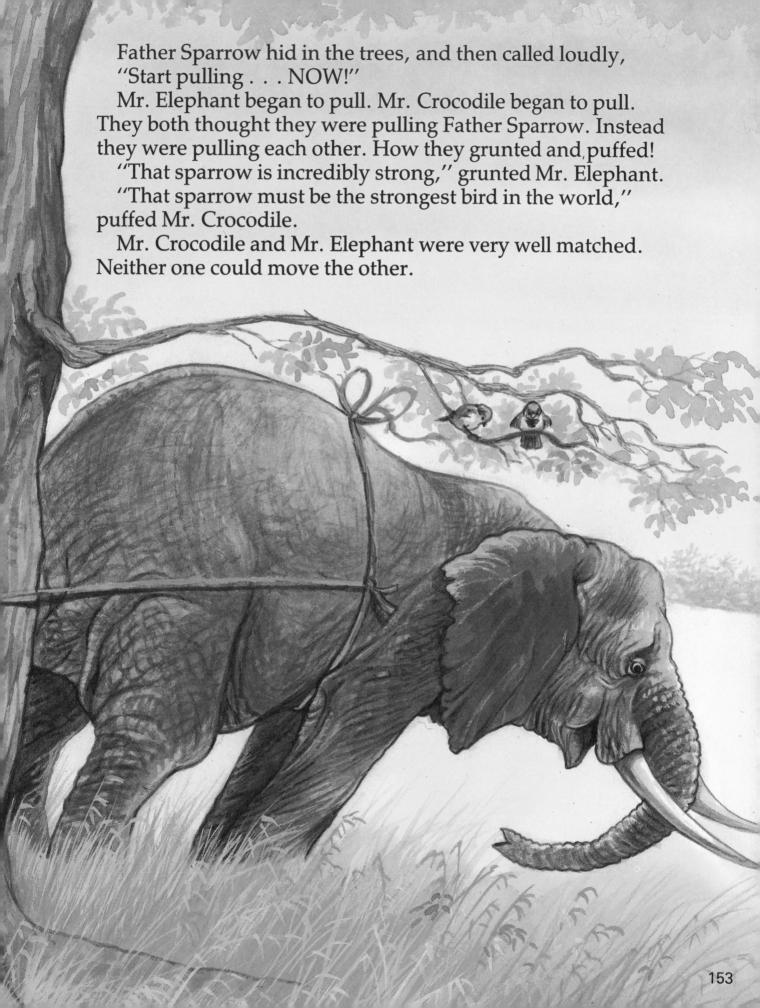

At sundown, Father Sparrow called from his hiding place.
"Are you ready to give in?"

"Yes . . . yes . . ." puffed Mr. Elephant. He was so tired.
He couldn't understand why Father Sparrow sounded so
fresh.

"Are you ready to give in?" called Father Sparrow again.

"Yes . . . yes . . ." grunted Mr. Crocodile. He was as tired
as Mr. Elephant. And he felt just as foolish.

"I'm letting go of the vine . . . NOW!" called Father
Sparrow. And as he said "NOW" he cut it through the
middle. Mr. Elephant lost his balance at one end and sat
down with a bump. Mr. Crocodile lost his balance at the other
end and slipped on the mud. They both disappeared into the
forest with the sound of laughter ringing in their ears. It
would be a long time before either of them were rude to
Father Sparrow again!

SING-LO AND THE DRAGON

Long ago, in a small village in China there was great excitement. A messenger from the great Emperor in Peking had called all the people into the village square, because he had something very important to tell them. They knew he came from the Emperor because he was dressed in fine silken robes and wore a hat with golden tassels. The two soldiers who stood beside him, blew a fanfare on their long curved horns when everyone was assembled. The crowd was silent as the old man was handed a scroll made of parchment. In a loud voice he began to read:

"The Emperor wishes it to be known that the Royal Dragon has escaped. There will be a big reward for anyone who can find him and an even bigger reward for anyone who is able to capture and return the Dragon to the Royal Palace."

When he had finished reading, he handed the scroll to one of his attendants who hung it up for everyone to see.

As the messenger left the village to spread the news, there was much talk among the people. It was well known that the Emperor kept a fierce, red dragon near the Palace gates to guard his many treasures. The thought of a fierce Dragon roaming about the streets frightened the people. They fled to their homes and locked the doors and windows.

At the end of the village, there lived an old woman with her grandson, Sing-Lo. She was old and did not go out into the village very often. Sing-Lo stopped on his way home from school so that he could listen to the Emperor's messenger and tell his grandmother. He heard the announcement with surprise; who would be able to catch a fire-breathing dragon or even get anywhere near one? Sing-Lo hurried home to practise flying his kite before supper, as there was going to be a prize given at school at the end of the week for the boy who could fly his kite the highest.

Soon he set off up the hill overlooking his home, singing merrily. He had quite forgotten all about the fierce red dragon as he climbed higher and higher in search of a good place for flying his kite.

Suddenly he became aware of being quite alone. He looked back down onto the village and there too, the streets were quiet and empty. Only then did he remember the words of the old man from the Emperor's Palace. He went on anyway, he couldn't see any Dragons about.

The evening was very warm and Sing-Lo sat down for a short rest. There were many caves nearby but Sing-Lo had never been inside them. A strange feeling came over him. He could sense he was not alone – someone was watching him. Turning round he could see two very large eyes looking at him from the darkness of one of the caves.

Sing-Lo nearly jumped out of his skin. Could this be the dragon, he wondered? "Who's there?" he whispered.

A gentle snort came from inside the cave and a deep voice said, "Don't be afraid. I am Kwang Fu, the Dragon and I've escaped from the Emperor's Palace. I'm tired of breathing fire all day and scaring everyone. I really want to be a friendly Dragon but no one will come anywhere near me."

"Oh!" cried Sing-Lo, feeling much happier. "May I be your friend? I don't know anything about dragons but I'm willing to learn."

Kwang Fu was so pleased he had found a friend to talk to that he forgot to breathe fire and came slowly out of the cave. He was so big that Sing-Lo took a few steps backwards.

"I ran away because I like it up here. I feel as free as the wind and I shall never, never return to the Palace. The only thing is – I do feel so very hungry. Have you anything in your pockets to eat?" said the Dragon.

"Sorry," said Sing-Lo, "but I can bring you something tomorrow. What would you like?"

"Big juicy oranges," snorted Kwang Fu. "I get so dry breathing fire. Oranges are the fruit I like best." He wagged his tail from side to side, knocking a couple of trees completely over as he did so.

Sing-Lo said, "Leave it to me," but he really didn't know how he was going to find enough oranges to feed a hungry dragon. He knew he would have to try. Then he remembered his friend who had a fruit stall in the market. Surely his friend would let him have some oranges at the end of the day.

159

Every evening that week, Sing-Lo went up the hillside to the cave with as many oranges as he could carry. He thought it best to say nothing to anyone about the Dragon, as Kwang Fu was determined to stay in the cave, but it would only be a matter of time before the Emperor's soldiers found him and took him back to the Palace.

"You can't stop here forever," said Sing-Lo on his next visit.

"I can, I can," said the Dragon. "As long as you bring me oranges," he added under his breath.

"What will you do when winter comes?" asked his friend, thinking he had caught him out.

"I can easily breathe fire and warm up the cave," said Kwang Fu.

Sing-Lo knew that he could not keep on coming to feed the dragon. His grandmother was beginning to ask questions about where he was going every evening. So he decided to go and see the Emperor's minister who was very pleased to have news of the dragon, at last. The Emperor had become very bad-tempered since Kwang Fu had escaped. You see, he was the only ruler who had his own red dragon to guard his treasures.

"Whatever can we do?" asked Sing-Lo.

"Well, now," said the minister, stroking his long white beard. "It seems to me that Kwang Fu is very lonely."

"Yes, yes," said Sing-Lo. "Perhaps you could ask the Emperor to find another dragon to keep him company, because he does need a friend."

The minister told the Emperor, who agreed, and very soon a young dragon was found and placed in the Palace grounds. Sing-Lo went to the cave to tell Kwang Fu.

"I shall NEVER, NEVER come down!" he stamped.

"Well, if you don't come down, no one will ever like you and you will never have another friend," said Sing-Lo. "Good-bye, Kwang Fu, I can't help you any more." He went away feeling very sad, because he had tried so hard to help his friend.

Kwang Fu felt very sad too, when Sing-Lo had gone. It would be nice to have a friend, and after all, it was lonely in the cave.

162

The next night, Kwang Fu crept back into the Palace grounds. Everyone was pleased to see him once more at the Royal Gates. The Emperor was smiling again and Sing-Lo was summoned to the Palace.

"I give you my word that there will always be plenty of oranges for the dragons," said the Emperor. "I feel sure they will soon become great friends. You are a very brave little fellow and I have a reward for you."

Sing-Lo and his grandmother were overjoyed at their rich reward and when he grew up, the Emperor made Sing-Lo Chief Keeper of Dragons at the Palace.

163

The Gingerbread Man

A little old man and a little old woman lived in a tiny cottage. Every day was the same because they had no children to play with or to make them laugh.

One day, the little old woman had an idea. It was such a splendid idea, she had to sit down and think about it. The little old man was sitting outside in the sun, so the little old woman said to herself, "I will make a little gingerbread man!"

She started mixing things, fat, sugar and eggs; then flour and ginger. She put in lots of ginger and made him a lovely dark brown. She rolled the dough and cut out the shape of a little man.

"Now, currants for his eyes and his buttons. Some lemon peel for his nose and his mouth . . . That's fine!"

She slid the gingerbread onto a baking sheet and put it into the oven to bake.

Later that morning, the little old woman heard a voice.

"Let me out! . . . Let me out!"

The voice came from the oven! Very carefully, she peeped inside. The Gingerbread Man leapt out!

"Wait!" she called. "Come back!" But he was off and running fast.

"Don't just sit there, little old man!" she cried. "Help me catch him!"

They ran after him.

"Stop! . . . Stop!" they shouted.

The Gingerbread Man grinned and called,

"Run, run as fast as you can
    You can't catch me
    I'm the Gingerbread Man."

And they couldn't!

A cow stood across his path. The Gingerbread Man ran between its legs.

"Mmm-ind your manners!" she mooed. "What are you doing?"

"I am running away!" laughed Gingerbread Man. "I have run away from the little old woman and the little old man, so I am running away from you!

    Run, run as fast as you can
    You can't catch me
    I'm the Gingerbread Man."

He was right. The cow could not catch him!

He raced past a horse trotting through a gate.
"Whoa!" called the horse. "Wait for me!"
Are you running away too?" cried the Gingerbread Man.
"Why not? . . Hee-hee-ee!" neighed the horse. "The
gate's open."
"I run away from everybody!" said the Gingerbread Man.
"I will run away from you too!

Run, run as fast as you can
You can't catch me
I'm the Gingerbread Man."

And even at a gallop the horse couldn't catch him.
Round the next bend he met a fox.
"Hallo!" called the fox. "Why, you are brown, just like me
. . . Look, we make a good pair."
The Gingerbread Man didn't stop. He ran faster and faster,
calling out, "I've run away from the little old woman, the little
old man, a cow AND a horse, so I can run away from you!

Run, run as fast as you can
You can't catch me
I'm the Gingerbread Man."

But . . . At last he stopped on the edge of a river.
"Oh!" said the Gingerbread Man. "I shall get wet . . . What
can I do?"

Up came the fox.

"You can sit on my tail, little brown friend. We will cross the river in no time."

So the Gingerbread Man climbed onto the fox's tail.

Soon the fox said, "Little friend, you will get wet on my tail. Jump on my back."

So the Gingerbread Man jumped onto the fox's back.

Half-way across the river the fox said, "Little friend, you are too heavy. Jump on my nose . . . You will be able to see better."

The Gingerbread Man laughed and jumped onto the fox's nose.

"This is fun!" he said.

When the fox had nearly reached the other side, he tossed his head. Up went the Gingerbread Man, spinning over and over in the air. Then . . . snap! snap! He was caught!

The fox gobbled him up and that was the end of the Gingerbread Man.

Rimski And The Weather-Vane

Rimski was a young rooster. He had golden feathers round his neck, tail feathers of shining green and a croaky voice which grew stronger every day. Each morning very early, he flapped up on to the yard gate. There he stretched his neck and his wings, trying out his 'Cock-a-doodle-doo!' . . . Yes, it was improving—reaching a high note.

After he had crowed, he stopped to listen, hoping someone would answer him.

One morning from a long way away came a faint 'Cock-a-doodle-doo!' That was a great day for Rimski. He strutted about feeling very proud.

One day, as he made his first crow, the church clock chimed. He hadn't noticed it before—it had just been mended. The sound annoyed him. It spoilt his own wonderful sound. Lifting his head to see where the strange sound had come from, he saw something shining at the top of the church spire. Then he looked again—and again! Was it possible?

A bird up there? . . . Yes, a golden one! . . . What did it mean by singing out that silly 'Ding-dong, ding-dong' rubbish! Why couldn't it give a proper 'Cock-a-doodle-doo'? This was serious. The matter needed his careful attention.

Pulling himself up tall, Rimski let out a loud and long 'Cock-a-doodle-doo!' He gave his feathers a shake, as if to say, "That should fix him!" . . . There was no answer. "Ha!" said Rimski. "He can't beat that!"

Later, the chimes went again, to be followed by 'Dong, dong, dong, dong, dongngng!' Rimski was very angry. It bothered him. What could he do? He couldn't sleep that night and through the hours he heard its chimes and its dongs. By morning he had made up his mind.

He'd go and see him—this 'Ding-dong Goldie' as he had nicknamed him. HE would make him change his tune!

Up on the gate, then out into the lane—Rimski strutted off. Mrs. Tabby Cat saw him as she sat washing herself.

"Good morning!" she called. "Going somewhere?"

"Of course!" answered Rimski. "I have important business to attend to. That bird up there—I'm going to put him in his place!" He tossed his head towards the church spire.

Mrs. Tabby glanced up: "That IS his place!" she said . . . Rimski ignored her.

Presently he came to a donkey, tethered on the grass.

"Hee-haw!" cried the donkey. "Could you please undo this rope? . . . I'd love to come for a walk!"

Rimski didn't even stop. "Sorry! I'm off to teach that bird a lesson!" . . .

"Which bird?" asked the donkey.

Once again Rimski tossed his head towards the church.

"Oh, he only does what the wind tells him," said the donkey.

"He'll do what I tell him!" boasted Rimski.

In the churchyard, he perched on a stone to give a loud 'Cock-a-doodle-doo!' No one answered.

Mrs. Blackbird came, searching for worms, then stopped to chat. Rimski explained why he had come; but she found it puzzling that he should want to quarrel with the weather-vane!

When the clock chimed again, Rimski was furious. "There, listen! I'll stop him—this weather-vane!"

Mrs. Blackbird said he would have to go up because weather-vanes never came down.

"How?" he asked.

"You could fly," she suggested. But Rimski made excuses so she took him to the steps. Up and up! Round and round! "Keep going!" she called. His head spun!

171

At last he came to a wide platform. The clock whirred—then blared out. Poor Rimski! It was terrifying! He found the workman's ladder fixed to the spire. Holding with his beak, he went up slowly. There was the bird. Golden? Yes: but no bird—just a metal shape. It swung round flinging Rimski off—far out into space.

He flapped and flapped! The ground looked miles away—then nearer and nearer! He was going to crash! A strong wind lifted him just in time. As it was, he flopped down—pitching on to his nose.

Mrs. Blackbird cheered him up. "What a flight, sir! You'll be famous!"

Rimski felt better. "Thank you, madam. I can certainly tell the world about Goldie up there. He's not real—only a painted thing going round and round!"

Mrs. Blackbird laughed. "Whichever way the wind blows, I suppose. HE can't make the sounds then! Could they come from the clock, d'you think!"

Rimski considered. "Possibly! . . . Possibly! Yes, you can take it from me—they came from the clock."

Mrs. Blackbird went on, "If we counted each dong would that tell us the time?"

Rimski tried to think. He couldn't keep up with this clever blackbird. The clock struck.

"Gracious!" she cried. "I must be off! Goodbye!"

Rimski stared after her, gave himself a shake and started for home.

The donkey asked how he'd got on. "Fine!" said Rimski. "That bird is just a weather-vane turning in the wind!" The donkey laughed.

Mrs. Tabby Cat opened one eye. "Anything exciting happen?" she asked.

"Of course!" he replied. "I climbed the spire, checked the clock and the weather-vane, then flew down!" . . . He flapped on to his gate. 'The cat's right!' he thought. Stretching up, Rimski gave his very best 'Cock-a-doodle-doo!'

GRUMBLYWITCH

Cherry Blossom Cottage was indeed a pretty place. There were roses growing round the door, the garden was neat and tidy and so was the cottage itself. Grumblywitch and her cat lived there. The cat's name was Odd because he had one green eye and one yellow one, which is not unusual when you belong to a witch! Poor Grumblywitch made life very hard for herself. She was never satisfied, nothing was ever good enough unless it was perfect. Everything had to be tidy in the cottage and the garden because she was so fussy.

Just now, she was over at Ritchie Willy the Cobbler's house, moving a swarm of bees from his newly-painted front door. The bees liked the yellow paint on Ritchie Willy's door much better than the tree trunk which was their home. Ritchie Willy wanted them to go away.

"Come bees, come away I say
   Buzzing, buzzing, come this way,"
commanded Grumblywitch.
The humming mass of bees on the
door parted to let the Queen Bee out.
She rose in the air and landed on the
top of the tall hat worn by
Grumblywitch. At the same time, all
the rest of the bees followed and
settled on her.

   "Are you alright?" asked Ritchie
Willy, because the witch's hat was a
solid mass of buzzing bees.

Grumblywitch did not answer
him. Getting on to her broomstick,
she rose straight up into the air and
whirled away over the trees. This
took the bees by surprise. They fell
off her hat but still followed her, like
a wisp of black smoke.

"Come with me, into my hive,
If you wish to stay alive,"
said Grumblywitch crossly to the
bees as she landed in her garden.
The Queen Bee was still sitting on
her hat, indeed, everything had
happened so quickly that the poor
thing did not know where she was.

Grumblywitch walked over to an
empty beehive by her potato patch
and spoke to the Queen and the
bees.

"Settle down and honey make
No more journeys will you take."
Quickly the bees swarmed and with
their Queen, buzzed into the
beehive.

Grumblywitch felt that she had
been a little cross with Ritchie Willy.
She had not even said goodbye to
him. Oh dear, she was getting so
grumpy and cross lately. As she
went into her cottage, Odd the cat,
ran out to her and wound his tail
round her legs.

"Mind what you do, cat," cried
Grumblywitch. "My feet hurt, I am
tired and I want to sit down." She
had forgotten her breakfast that
morning and her stomach rumbled
and grumbled, as she was beginning
to feel very hungry. The cat said
rather cheekily.

"Witch Grumbly? Grumblywitch?
Witch Rumbly! Rumblywitch!"

"Odd is right, I *am* 'grumblyrumbly' and oh, how my poor feet hurt," said Grumblywitch as she put on the kettle to make some tea. This, and taking off her boots made her feel better. Her feet were her problem and that is a terrible thing for a witch. Her witch's boots pinched her feet, but she could not go out of her cottage without them. She had to wear them when she had work to do, no matter how much they hurt.

Grumblywitch gave the cat a saucer of milk and stroked him gently. Grumblywitch might be her name but she was not grumpy really, it was just that her feet made her cross. She filled a bowl with warm water, poured herself a cup of tea and put the bowl on the floor. She put her aching feet down into the warm water.

Just then, Ritchie Willy walked in through the door. When Grumblywitch came home feeling tired and cross, she had not closed it properly. Odd the cat, ran to greet him because they were very good friends and he was pleased to see him.

Grumblywitch was not so pleased. How terrible that Ritchie Willy should see her soaking her feet. If she had not been in such a hurry to get her boots off, she would not have forgotten to close the door.

"Grit and gravel," she said crossly to herself. She would have to stay where she was, she could not do anything else.

"You moved those bees, it was so kind. Your door was open . . . I hope you do not mind." Ritchie Willy stopped speaking as he saw Grumblywitch glaring at him. Indeed, he was greatly concerned because being a cobbler, the boots and shoes that people wore were his trade. Oh dear me, he thought as he saw her poor swollen feet. Now he knew why the witch had been off in such a hurry.

"Dear witch," he said. "It was so good of you to rid me of those tiresome bees. You left my garden before I had time to ask what I could do for you in return. You are always doing things for me."

Feeling so ashamed of herself, Grumblywitch felt a 'humblywitch'. How could she have been so cross with such a nice old man?

"How good of you to come," she said. "I am sorry I went off like that. It is no use pretending, Ritchie Willy, my feet are very sore. What can I do?"

Ritchie Willy knew exactly how he could repay her kindness. He could see that her boots were much too small. It was easy to help her, he would make her a new pair of boots.

"Please will you let me make you a new pair of boots, just like these, but in a size which will be more comfortable?" he asked.

Both Grumblywitch and the cat were very pleased. Happy days would be here again for them if her feet were better. So she accepted and when she had dried her feet, Ritchie Willy measured them carefully and, bidding her goodbye, went back to his cottage.

Ritchie Willy worked all through the night and early the next morning, he left the boots outside the cottage door.

When Grumblywitch opened the
door to let Odd out, she found a
lovely new pair of soft, black,
elastic-sided boots. She tried them
on at once. They were perfect. They
were so comfortable that she did a
little hop, skip and a jump.

Her stomach made its usual rumbly noise, reminding her that neither
she nor the cat had eaten any breakfast yet. She made some tea and gave
Odd some milk. This time she made herself hot buttered toast and
enjoyed it. Then she and Odd sat in front of the fire feeling very happy
and contented.

"I'll go and see my sisters, that is what I will do,
    Riding my broomstick . . . and I'll take you,"
Grumblywitch told Odd. That was a good idea, for it was many moons
since she had seen Bumblywitch and Fumblywitch. They might notice her
lovely new boots and as she did not feel cross anymore they might notice
that too!

So Grumblywitch and her cat Odd, flew away on her broomstick over
the trees.

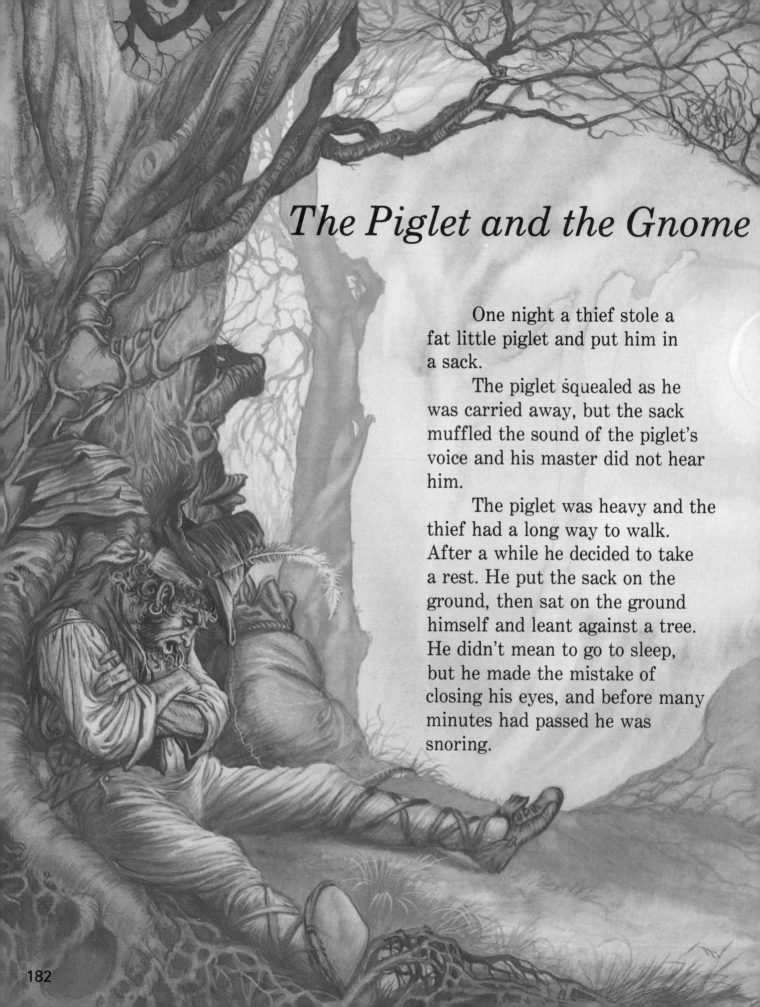

The Piglet and the Gnome

One night a thief stole a fat little piglet and put him in a sack.

The piglet squealed as he was carried away, but the sack muffled the sound of the piglet's voice and his master did not hear him.

The piglet was heavy and the thief had a long way to walk. After a while he decided to take a rest. He put the sack on the ground, then sat on the ground himself and leant against a tree. He didn't mean to go to sleep, but he made the mistake of closing his eyes, and before many minutes had passed he was snoring.

The fat little piglet did
not like being in the sack. He
squealed and fidgeted and wriggled.
He huffed and he puffed and he
squirmed. Now it so happened
that the thief had put the sack
right near a hole where a
gnome had his house. The gnome
was nearly deafened when the
piglet squealed, and nearly
tipped out of bed by all the
fidgeting and wriggling. He
went outside to see what was
causing the disturbance.

He untied the sack and looked inside.

"Hallo," he said. "What are you doing in there?"

"I've been stolen," said the piglet. "I don't like it in here. I want to go home."

"And so you shall," said the gnome who could understand pig talk perfectly well. He helped the piglet out of the sack and sent him on his way.

Then, because he liked having a bit of fun, the gnome got into the sack himself and waited for the thief to wake up, which he did, a little while later.

The thief hoisted the sack onto his shoulder and set off along a dark lane. He whistled to himself, and thought about all the things he could do with the piglet he had in his sack.

There was another gnome sitting in one of the trees in the lane. He was a friend of the gnome in the sack. He knew his friend was about because he had heard him talking to the piglet, but he couldn't see him.

"Where are you Dick?" he called.

The thief nearly jumped out of his skin. He looked all around. There was no sign of anyone, that he could see. 'I must be imagining things,' he thought. And then, before he had recovered from his fright, he heard another voice. A voice that came from just behind his right ear.

"I'm in the sack
Riding pig-a-back!"

The thief felt his hair stand on end. He thought the piglet was still in the sack. After all, hadn't he put it there himself? He dropped the sack. . .and he ran. He wanted nothing to do with a talking piglet. It would tell the whole world it had been stolen and who had stolen it.

"There goes someone who will never dare to steal another piglet," laughed the gnomes as the thief disappeared into the distance.

Jonathan John Has A Lazy Day

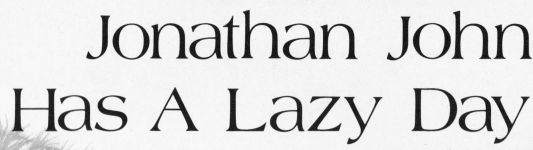

Jonathan John had built himself a house on a hilly slope. It had a turf roof on which daisies and buttercups grew and a chimney made of stone. He built a shed for his cow and a sty for his pig. And then he asked the girl with the rosy cheeks and long yellow plaits to be his wife.

Gertrude made the little house snug inside. She cooked, she cleaned and she polished. She looked after the cow and the pig and she churned the butter. When the baby was born, she looked after him too. And every day, when the sun was overhead, she carried Jonathan's dinner to him in the field.

At the end of one summer's day, when the sun had made Jonathan feel hot and tired, and when his fingers were sore with weeding, he came home with an attack of the grumbles.

"You are very lucky, wife," he said to Gertrude.

"Why is that?" asked Gertrude. She was hot and tired too.

"Because you can stay at home all day and play with the baby," said Jonathan enviously.

"But I churn the butter, and look after the cow and the pig. I cook. I clean . . ."

Jonathan interrupted her. "You don't call that work, do you? Work is weeding and hoeing and raking. It seems very unfair to me that one of us should do all the work while the other does no work at all."

Jonathan grumbled and grumbled, and Gertrude decided that he would have to be taught a lesson before he turned the milk sour!

"Let's change places, just for one day," she said. "Tomorrow I will work in the field and you can stay at home."

Jonathan was quick to agree. Now Gertrude would find out for herself how hard he worked and how unfair it all was.

Next morning, Gertrude gave him a long list of instructions . . . don't wake the baby, boil the porridge, churn the butter, take the cow to pasture, don't let the pig escape from the sty, bring me my dinner . . . and then she went to the field.

"What a lazy day I am going to have," said Jonathan. As soon as Gertrude had gone, he stretched himself in a chair and went to sleep. He woke after an hour and began to churn the butter. Churning soon made his arm ache. It made him thirsty too.

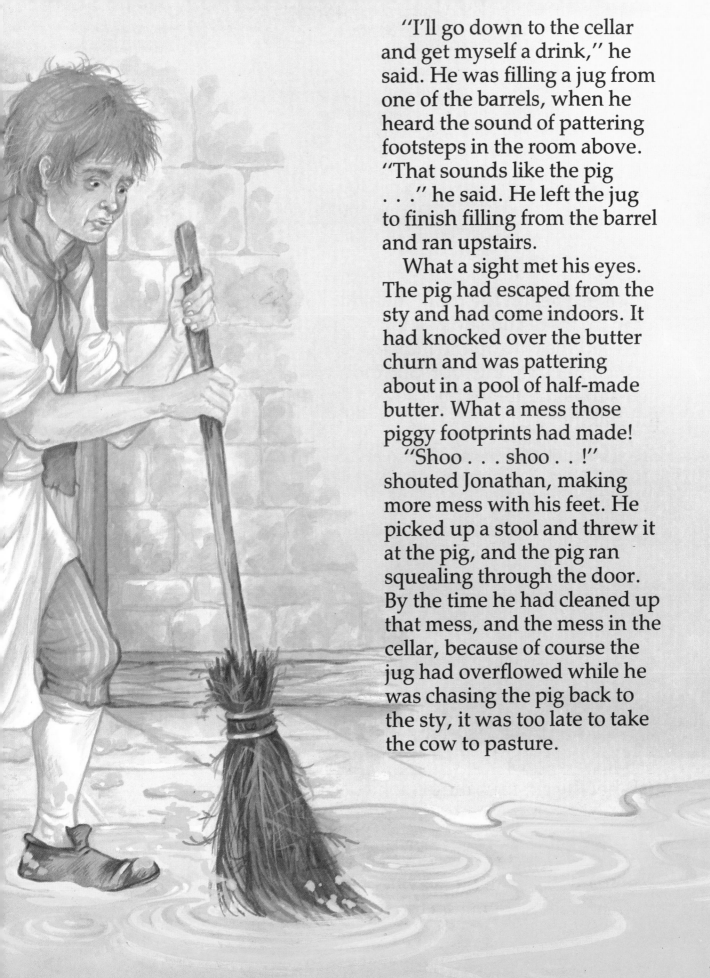

"I'll go down to the cellar and get myself a drink," he said. He was filling a jug from one of the barrels, when he heard the sound of pattering footsteps in the room above. "That sounds like the pig . . ." he said. He left the jug to finish filling from the barrel and ran upstairs.

What a sight met his eyes. The pig had escaped from the sty and had come indoors. It had knocked over the butter churn and was pattering about in a pool of half-made butter. What a mess those piggy footprints had made!

"Shoo . . . shoo . . !" shouted Jonathan, making more mess with his feet. He picked up a stool and threw it at the pig, and the pig ran squealing through the door. By the time he had cleaned up that mess, and the mess in the cellar, because of course the jug had overflowed while he was chasing the pig back to the sty, it was too late to take the cow to pasture.

"I'll put her on the roof," he said. "She can't come to any harm up there and she will find plenty to eat."

He led the cow up the hilly slope beside the house and pushed her onto the roof. She didn't like it very much. He tied a rope round her middle and dropped the long end down the chimney.

When he got back indoors, he tied the rope round his own waist. Now the cow couldn't possibly stray without him knowing.

"How much cleverer I am than Gertrude," he said. "Fancy walking the cow all the way to pasture, as she does, when there is grass growing on the roof."

190

He put the porridge pot on the fire, checked that the baby was still asleep, which he was, in spite of all the noise that had been going on, and sat down. He was surprised how tired he felt and it wasn't long before he was snoring. He woke very suddenly and was astonished to find himself half-way up the chimney, with no idea of how he had got there.

The answer was really simple. The cow wasn't used to grazing in such a small space, or one so high up. She had got too close to the edge of the roof and had fallen off. The rope saved her, but now she was dangling in mid-air, half-way between the roof and the ground! Because Jonathan and the cow were tied to different ends of the same rope, when the cow went DOWN, Jonathan couldn't do anything else but go UP. And that was how they stayed until Gertrude came home.

"Oh you poor cow," she cried when she saw the cow dangling in the air. She quickly cut the rope and the cow dropped to the ground with a grateful moo. There was a cry and a splash from within the house.

"Oh you poor man," laughed Gertrude as she helped Jonathan out of the porridge pot, for of course as soon as Gertrude cut the rope to release the cow, there was only one way Jonathan could go, and that was DOWN. He fell straight into the porridge pot! What a good thing it was that the fire had gone out and the porridge was cold.

"Tomorrow," said Jonathan, when Gertrude had washed the porridge from his face and kissed the end of his nose, "I will go to the field. You can stay at home. Too many things go wrong when I stay at home."

DESMOND THE DRAGON

It was a beautiful morning. A pale wintry sun was just rising over the hills. King Gustav decided that he could not stay in bed a moment longer. For once, he would be up before the servants and take a walk in his lovely Castle grounds.

The King struggled with the great iron bars on the Castle door. It would be so good to breathe the fresh morning air. He pulled the doors wide . . . and gave a cry of terror! The beautiful morning was spoilt for there, sitting on his very doorstep, was Desmond the Dragon.

King Gustav was a brave man and a good man. His kingdom was a happy contented place. There was only one thing that spoilt life for King Gustav and his subjects . . . Desmond the Dragon. Desmond the Dragon was the terror of Gustavia. He would storm through the growing wheat fields flattening all before him. Sometimes at night, he breathed flashing fire which burned barns, farmhouses and cottages. No one was safe and no one knew when he would strike.

Now, on this fine sunny morning, the dragon was sitting boldly on the Castle steps. Swiftly, King Gustav reached up to ring the giant alarm bell on the wall. To his amazement, before he could touch it, Desmond, the Dragon sank slowly to his knees. He began to make strange whining sounds, and King Gustav turned to stare at him as he had never heard Desmond do this before.

It was then that King Gustav noticed the baby dragon. It was crouched, shivering beside Desmond, almost hidden behind the enormous creature. The sight of the tiny dragon startled the King and he wondered why Desmond was on his knees making such a pitiful noise.

King Gustav took his hand down from the bell and turned to face his old enemy.

Desmond spoke, "Have mercy, have mercy, good King Gustav. I have come to offer myself to work in your service, if you will save the life of my baby son."

King Gustav could hardly believe his ears. Was this really the fiercest of dragons begging for mercy? Was this some trick? Did the Dragon mean to set fire to his castle as soon as his back was turned? King Gustav was not sure. At that moment, the baby dragon crept right up to the hem of his robe, curled itself up on the warm velvet and fell asleep.

King Gustav was touched as he looked down at the little, sleeping creature. He looked up at Desmond and waited for him to explain.

"His mother died two days ago," said Desmond. "I cannot bring up a baby by myself. If you will care for my son, here in the Castle, I will change my ways and become a good dragon."

King Gustav was a very kind man. He felt he just could not refuse. It would not be easy, but they would look after the baby and Desmond would have his chance.

From that day onwards the King led the Dragon round the Castle grounds on a pair of reins, just like a lead. "Sit!" he would command, and Desmond would flop down in a great heap. "Wait!" he would say, and the Dragon stayed still for hours. Later, let off his lead, Desmond learnt to 'Fetch,' 'Drop,' and 'Beg.' The huge creature would trot everywhere at King Gustav's heels for all the world like a tame hound dog. He slept each night in one of the barns.

Meanwhile, the servants in the Royal nursery had named the baby dragon, Benjamin. They taught him to be good and polite, and so it was that before long, the two dragons almost became part of the family.

Of course, Benjamin was now growing fast. One day, King Gustav decided that Desmond should visit his son at bedtime each evening. The Queen would read a bedtime story to both dragons sitting by the great fire in the Castle hall.

When Benjamin was led off to bed, Desmond would return to sleep in the barn. King Gustav began to notice how Desmond always turned to look with sad, longing eyes at the flames flickering in the fire.

King Gustav knew why the fire made Desmond unhappy. A Dragon is proud because he is able to breathe fire. Since coming to live in the Castle, Desmond had really changed his ways. There was no doubt about it, thought the King, dragons do have a right to be fierce and Desmond had learnt his lessons well. He deserved some reward. . . .

So, one evening, after the stories were read, King Gustav did not send Desmond back to the barn.

"I have an important job for you, Desmond," said the King. "You have become a very responsible Dragon. I am going to make you Keeper of the King's Candles."

Desmond looked as if he could not believe his ears. Candles had bright, flickering flames, the flames he loved. Whatever did the King want him to do? King Gustav explained, "Each night about this time, every candle in the castle has to be lit . . . every single one . . . from the largest in the hall to the smallest on the cellar stairs. Whenever we have parties, many more candles will be needed. It's just the job for you, Desmond. You can light each candle with a flash of fire and I shall be pleased for you to do it."

Desmond was delighted. He could be a real dragon again, and when Benjamin grew older, he could help him. Together they would be Keepers of the King's Candles for ever and ever. He leapt into the air with a great roar, crying out, "I must be the luckiest dragon alive."

"Sit!" King Gustav called out with a smile. At once the huge creature was there by his side. "Yes, you are a lucky dragon, and such a well behaved one too," the King told him, patting his scaly head fondly.

Desmond the Dragon turned bright pink with pride.

The Shepherdess and the Sweep

Once there was a shepherdess. Not a real shepherdess but a delicate porcelain one. She was very beautiful. She stood beside the porcelain sweep, on a table, in a dark and crowded parlour. The sweep was as black as coal, except for his face which was as pink and as clean as the shepherdess's own. Just behind them stood the Chinese mandarin. He had a black stubby pig-tail hanging down his back, and grey slanting eyes. The Chinese mandarin nodded all the time. He couldn't help it. It was the way he was made. The shepherdess called him Grand-father, though he wasn't, because if he had been she would have been Chinese too, and she wasn't.

On the far side of the room and facing the table where the three porcelain figures stood, was a carved wooden cabinet. Carved in the very middle of the door was a very peculiar man. He had a lop-sided smile that was hardly a smile at all, and a beard, and legs like a goat. The children who lived in the house and some-times came into the parlour called him Mr. Goat-legged, Commanding General, Private, Sergeant, because they thought it suited him, though if they were in a hurry they called him Mr. Goat-legs.

199

One day, Mr. Goat-legs asked the Chinese mandarin if he could marry the shepherdess. The Chinese mandarin nodded, as was his habit.

"Good," said Mr. Goat-legs looking pleased.

"But Grandpa, I don't want to marry horrid Mr. Goat-legs," said the shepherdess.

"It is too late now. I have given my consent," said the Chinese mandarin. "The wedding will be tonight. Wake me up in time for the ceremony." And with no more ado, he nodded himself to sleep.

The little shepherdess cried tears that looked like seed pearls. The sweep tried to comfort her.

"Please take me away from the parlour and out into the wide world," she pleaded. "I cannot marry Mr. Goat-legs."

The running stags carved on the side of the cabinet saw them climbing down to the floor.

"The shepherdess and the sweep are eloping!" they cried.

The mandarin woke with a start and began nodding so furiously, his whole body rocked backwards and forwards. The shepherdess and the sweep had never seen him so angry and were very frightened.

"There is only one way to escape," whispered the sweep. "We must go into the stove and up the chimney to the roof."

It was a difficult climb, even for the sweep. It was dark, and sooty, and steep. The shepherdess was so afraid she would slip. If she fell she knew she would break into a thousand pieces.

"Do not look down," whispered the sweep as he followed behind and guided her feet to the nooks and crannies. "Look up towards the star which shines at the end of our journey."

When the shepherdess looked up through the dark tunnel of the chimney, she could see a tiny speck of light, far, far away in the distance. The higher they climbed the bigger it grew, and when they got to the top it became the entire sky.

The shepherdess and the sweep sat side by side on the rim of the chimney-pot and looked wearily across the rooftops at the wide, wide world. The shepherdess did not like what she saw. The big wide world was so very big, and so very wide. She began to cry again.

"Please take me back to the parlour," she sobbed. "I like the big wide world even less than I like Mr. Goat-legs." Her face was soon stained with sooty tears. The little sweep could not bear to see her so unhappy and agreed to take her back.

The journey down the chimney was just as difficult as the journey up had been. It was just as dark. Just as frightening. When they finally crawled out of the stove and into the parlour they were met by a strange and eerie silence.

"Something has happened!" cried the shepherdess. "Oh I just know something dreadful has happened!"

It had. In his anger, the Chinese mandarin had rolled off the edge of the table and now he was lying in pieces on the floor.

"Oh dear, it's all our fault," cried the shepherdess. "Oh poor Grandpa . . . what are we to do?" And she cried even more.

"We can't do anything," said the sweep, "but don't worry. Someone is sure to come along and glue him together again."

And someone did. But from that day onwards he lost his habit of nodding. It didn't matter how many times Mr. Goat-legs asked if he could still marry the shepherdess, the Chinese mandarin, would not, could not, nod and give his consent. And so the shepherdess and the sweep were able to stand side by side until the end of their days.

Little Red Hen

Little Red Hen strutted out of the farmyard and into Farmer Brown's big field. The wheat had been cut and gathered so she could scratch about anywhere.

"I might find some ears of wheat that the farmer's men have dropped," she clucked.

And she did. They were fine fat ones, full of golden grains. She carried them back to the farmyard to show her friends.

"Cluck, cluck!" called Little Red Hen. "Will you help me plant these grains?"

"Oh, No-o-!" yawned Ginger Cat. "I'm too sleee-py." Ginger Cat went up on to the roof of the barn and went to sleep.

"Oh, No-o-!" squeaked Grey Rat. "I am busy storing winter food in the barn." Grey Rat scampered away.

"Oh, No-o!" grunted Pink Pig. "I am off to find some acorns." She trotted away into the trees.

"Very well," said Little Red Hen. "I will plant them myself."

And she did. She put them in fine straight rows. She watched the rows every day. She saw green shoots peeping up out of the ground. Then she saw the wheat at the top begin to ripen in the sunshine. Little Red Hen was pleased.

"My wheat is ready!" called Little Red Hen to the animals. "Will you help me gather it?"

"Not today," said Ginger Cat. "I must wash my fur."

"Don't count on me," squeaked Grey Rat. "My work is never done."

"You can see I'm too busy," grunted Pink Pig. "I have ten piglets to feed!"

"Very well," said Little Red Hen. "I will gather it myself."

And she did. She snipped each stalk and made a neat bundle.

"That's done!" she clucked. "Will you help me carry the wheat to the miller? The miller will grind it into flour."

"Impossible!" said Ginger Cat, opening one eye.

"Quite impossible!" squeaked Grey Rat.

"Quite, quite impossible!" grunted Pink Pig.

"Very well," said Little Red Hen, "I will carry it myself."

And she did. She carried it all the way to the mill. The great stones at the mill turned round and round, grinding the grain into flour. When the flour was fine enough, the miller put it into a linen bag.

"Thank you," said Little Red Hen.

When she came back to the farmyard, Little Red Hen called out, "Here is the flour . . . Who will help me take it to the baker to be made into bread?"

"Out of the question," said Ginger Cat, walking away.

"Quite out of the question," squeaked Grey Rat, running off.

"Quite, quite out of the question," grunted Pink Pig. "I am too fat to go anywhere."

"I suppose 'out of the question' means 'No'," said Little Red Hen. "I will take it myself."

And she did. She went to the baker and brought back a crusty loaf.

"Who will help me eat this lovely new bread?" she clucked. The animals all gathered around.

"I will!" said Ginger Cat, twitching his whiskers.

"So will I!" squeaked Grey Rat. "I am so hungry."

"Don't forget me!" grunted Pink Pig. "It looks delicious!"

"It is delicious," said Little Red Hen, "but you didn't help me at all . . . so it is quite out of the question for you to have any of it! Cluck! Cluck!"

THREE GOLDEN HAIRS

Once there was a poor man whose only son was born under a lucky star. It was foretold that, one day, he would marry the King's daughter.

The King was very cross when he heard the news. "A poor boy like that marry my daughter! NEVER!" he said. He went to see the boy's father.

"I want to buy your son," he said.

The King was told the boy was not for sale, but he nagged, and argued, and pleaded, till at last the boy's father thought, 'My son can come to no harm with the King. He will give him a better life than I can. . .I must let him go.'

The King carried the baby off. But instead of taking him home to the palace, he put him in a box and cast the box adrift on the river. With any luck it would float out to sea and the baby would never be seen again. Marry his daughter indeed!

The boy hadn't been born under a lucky star for nothing. The box was fished from the river by a miller. He took the baby home to his wife and they brought him up as their own son. He grew into a fine strong lad, full of mischief, but kind too.

One day, the King happened, just by chance, to call at the mill.

"What a handsome boy," said the King. "Is he your son?"

"Oh that he was," sighed the miller fondly. "We found him, as a baby, floating down the river in a box."

The King went pale. He called for pen and paper and quickly wrote a letter which he sealed with bright red wax.

"Can you spare the boy to carry this letter to the Queen?" he asked the miller. "It is very urgent."

"Jack will be honoured to carry your letter," said the miller, little knowing that the King had written 'Kill the bearer of this letter. Will explain when I get home.'

Jack set off immediately. Towards nightfall he knocked at a cottage door and asked for shelter for the night.

"This is the home of a band of robbers," said an old woman who answered. "Are you sure you want to stay?"

"I am carrying a letter to the Queen. They will not harm me," said Jack. He was asleep when the robbers returned so he did not see them open the letter.

"Look at this!" they said. "Now isn't that just disgraceful. Kill a nice lad like that . . . we'll soon settle this." They wrote a new letter which said, 'Marry the bearer of this letter to our daughter', and fixed the King's seal so that it looked as though it had never been broken. They burnt the letter the King had written.

Jack continued his journey next day without knowing that the letter had been changed. He was very pleased to marry the Princess when the Queen arranged it.

When the King returned and found he had a new son-in-law he was very angry. "If you want to stay married to my daughter you must bring me three golden hairs from the head of the giant," he thundered, thinking secretly that the giant would soon put an end to Jack.

Jack set off at once. The guard at the gate of the first city he passed through asked him if he knew why the fountain in the market place had run dry. "I will give you an answer when I return," said Jack. The guard at the gate of another city asked Jack if he knew why a tree which had once borne golden apples no longer bore even a leaf. "I will have an answer for you when I return," said Jack.

The ferryman who took him across the lake asked how he could escape from the ferryboat and gain his liberty. Once again, Jack said he would give an answer on his return.

When Jack reached the giant's cave, the giant was not at home. "What do you want from him?" asked the giant's grandmother.

"Nothing very much," said Jack boldly. "Just three golden hairs from his head."

The giant's grandmother frowned. "That could be very risky," she said. "I'd better help you. But first you must hide." She turned Jack into an ant and hid him in her apron.

While they were waiting for the giant to come home Jack asked the grandmother if she knew why the city fountain had run dry.

"I do not," she said, "But I'll ask the giant if he knows."

"Will you also ask him why the tree which used to bear golden apples bears them no longer, and what the ferryman must do to gain his liberty?" asked Jack.

"I can smell boy!" said the giant when he got home. "Where is he?" But Jack was well hidden and the giant wanted his supper so he soon gave up looking.

After he had eaten the giant lay his head in his grandmother's lap and went to sleep. It wasn't long before he was snoring.

The grandmother tweeked one of the golden hairs from the giant's head.

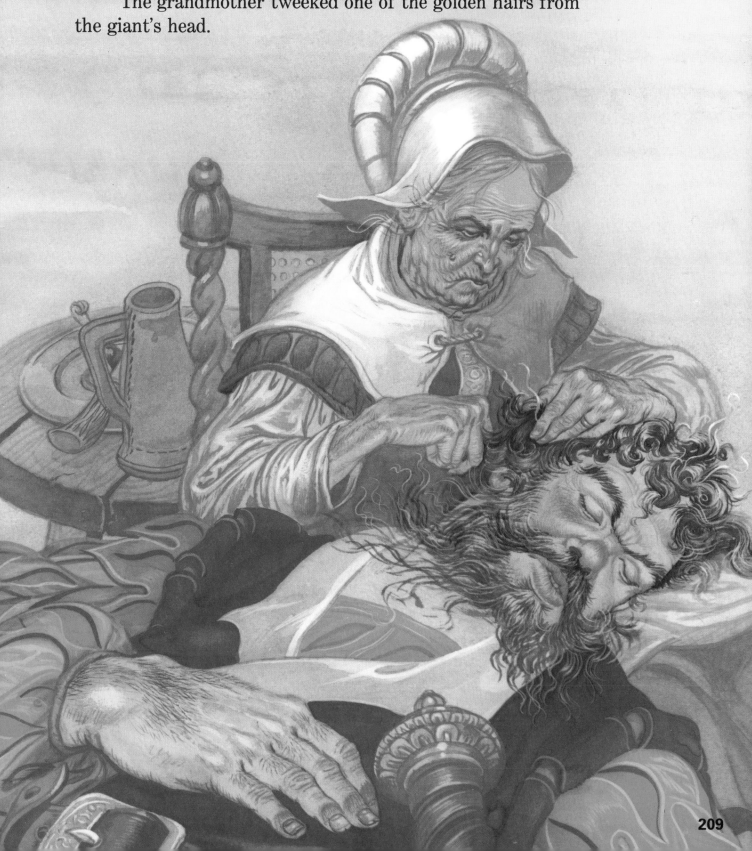

"What was that?" cried the giant, waking up with a start.

"Nothing dear," said the giant's grandmother. "I was dreaming of a fountain which has run dry. Why would a fountain run dry dear?"

"Because there is a toad sitting under it," said the giant who knew the answer to almost everything. "Kill the toad and the water will flow again."

As soon as the giant closed his eyes the giant's grandmother tweeked out another of his hairs.

"Ouch!" cried the giant. "What was that?"

"Nothing dear," said the giant's grandmother. "I had another dream, that was all. Now why should an apple tree that used to bear golden apples bear them no longer?"

"There is a mouse gnawing at the root. Kill the mouse and the tree will bear fruit again," yawned the giant sleepily.

The giant's grandmother thought it better to wait a while before she pulled out the third hair.

"Ouch!" said the giant when she did. "I suppose you've had another dream?"

"Yes, I have. How did you guess?" she asked. "Now tell me, what must the ferryman do to gain his liberty?"

"Give the rudder to another passenger of course," sighed the giant. "Now will you let me get some sleep?"

"Of course dear. I won't disturb you again, I promise," she said.

The next day, when the giant's grandmother had turned Jack into himself, he set off for home.

Jack waited until he was safely across the lake before he told the ferryman how he could gain his liberty and when he answered the questions the city guards had asked, he was richly rewarded with gold and silver.

The King had to smile and pretend to be pleased when he saw Jack, for not only had Jack brought the three hairs, he was now very rich. The Princess really was pleased to see him.

It so happened that the King himself was the next person to cross the lake. The ferryman handed him the rudder. The King is ferrying passengers to this day, which probably serves him right. Perhaps, one day, Jack will tell him what he told the ferryman.

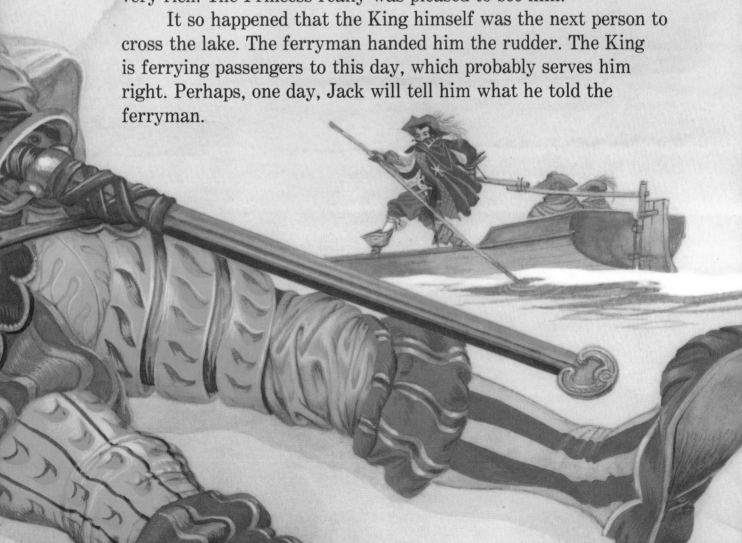

A Singing Lesson

Fred Frog had a deep baritone voice and he liked to sing.

"Please sing me a song, Fred," Freda Frog would say. Fred would first find a place to sit and then he would wobble his chin and serenade her with the croakiest of croaks.

"Oh Fred, that is beautiful," Freda would say, her own voice full of admiration. Whereupon Fred would swell with pride and wobble his chin harder and sing louder, and longer, and hardly stop to take breath at all. But though Freda liked to hear Fred sing, there were those who thought his voice sounded like a rusty old hinge on a broken-down door.

One day, when Fred was singing, Reggie Reed-Warbler called: "Hey Fred, where's your oil can?"

"I should take some singing lessons if I were you," called Wally Wagtail.

"We can't hear OURSELVES sing with that racket going on," called the curlews.

"You sound like a cornflake with a sore throat," said the meadow-pipit.

The underneath part of Fred's chin stopped wobbling and his lip started to wobble instead. His feelings were hurt.

"Take no notice," said Freda. "They only say those things because they are jealous of your beautiful voice."

"Jealous of HIS voice," laughed the birds. "When we have such beautiful voices of our own? Don't be silly . . . now boys, let's show those frogs what real singing is all about."

The birds whistled and sang and filled the sky and the wind with the beautiful sounds that only birds can make. Poor Fred. A tear rolled down his cheek. He slid noiselessly into the water and hid in the mud on the bottom of the pond.

"Please don't cry," said Freda as she sidled into the mud beside him. "Your voice is the most beautiful voice in the world to me."

"If only I could sing like a bird," sighed Fred. "If only I could whistle and trill." And no matter what Freda said, Fred would not come out of the mud.

"Where's Fred?" asked Reggie Reed-Warbler next morning.

"You have hurt his feelings because you laughed at him," said Freda. "You have made him ashamed of his own voice and now he wishes he could sing like you."

Reggie Reed-Warbler thought for a moment. The birds hadn't meant to be unkind to Fred. "If he wants to sing like a bird, then we will teach him," he said. "Go and fetch him, Freda."

Freda really did prefer Fred's voice the way it was, but she went and got him all the same because she knew that was what Fred would have wanted. Fred came up and sat beside her on a lily-pad and waited for his lesson to begin. The birds sat in the reeds facing him.

"This shouldn't take long," said Reggie.

Fred concentrated very hard. He really did. First Reggie showed him how to sing. Then Wally tried. And then all the other birds tried. Still Fred's voice did nothing but croak and creak and groan.

"No . . . no . . . Not like that," said Reggie for the hundredth time as yet another peculiar squeaky croak came from Fred's throat.

"I'm trying . . . I really am," said Fred.

"He is . . ." said Freda. "I can tell."

"You're being stubborn," shouted Reggie at last. "You don't want to sing like a bird."

"But I do . . . I do . . ." sobbed Fred. His poor green face looked back at him from the water. His tears plopped like pebbles and made his reflection disappear.

Tired and exasperated though the birds were, they began to feel sorry for him.

"Do cheer up," they said. "It's not your fault you can't sing like a bird."

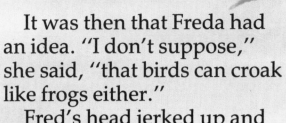

It was then that Freda had an idea. "I don't suppose," she said, "that birds can croak like frogs either."

Fred's head jerked up and his tears stopped.

"Of course they can," said Reggie.

"Let's hear you then," said Freda.

The birds tried, they really did, but the sounds that came from their throats as they tried to croak like frogs were as strange as the sounds that came from Fred's throat when he tried to sing like a bird.

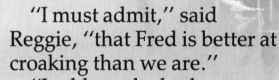

"I must admit," said Reggie, "that Fred is better at croaking than we are."

"I told you he had a beautiful voice," said Freda.

"I suppose he has, for a frog," admitted Reggie.

And that was how it ended, for after all, who wants to listen to a bird who croaks like a frog, or a frog who sings like a bird. A frog is a frog and a bird is a bird. Frogs croak, birds whistle, and that's the way it should be.

217

Pixie Visitors

Pixies enjoy getting together and having fun. The trouble with pixies is, they always hold their parties at night when ordinary people are trying to sleep.

Once, there was a farmer and his wife. They had no one to help them on the farm and were always very tired at the end of the day. When the last chore was done they would put an extra log on the fire to keep it glowing through the night and go straight to bed.

One cold dark night, when there was frost on the hedgerow and icicles hanging from the roof, a pixie face peeped through the farmhouse window. The pixie took one look at the empty kitchen and the glowing fire and sent out a message. Before many minutes had passed the farmhouse kitchen was as crowded with pixies as a railway station is crowded with people in the rush hour.

It wouldn't have mattered if the pixies had had their fun quietly. But they didn't. Having fun to a pixie means squealing and shouting and screeching and singing. It means rattling and banging and slamming and clanking and popping. It means stamping and clapping. It means making a HULLABALOO!!! No one can sleep through it. Not even a tired farmer and his tired wife.

"Who is making all that noise?" cried the farmer's wife, sitting up in bed and pressing her hands to her ears.

"There are pixies playing in the kitchen," said the farmer who was on his hands and knees peeping through a hole in the floor.

"Then tell them to go and play somewhere else," grumbled his wife.

"I can't do that," said the farmer. And he was right! He couldn't! If he offended the pixies there was no telling what they might do. There are so many things on a farm that a pixie can make go wrong. They can curdle the milk and stop the hens laying for a start. If they are really annoyed they can make EVERYTHING go wrong.

"We'll just have to put up with the noise," sighed the farmer.

The farmhouse kitchen was warm and cosy and the pixies liked it so much they began to come EVERY night. The farmer and his wife hardly slept at all. They grew more and more tired. They just couldn't stop yawning during the day. When the farmer's wife fell asleep in the hen house and dropped all the eggs she had been collecting, the farmer decided the time had come to do something. But what? Offend the pixies and they were in trouble.

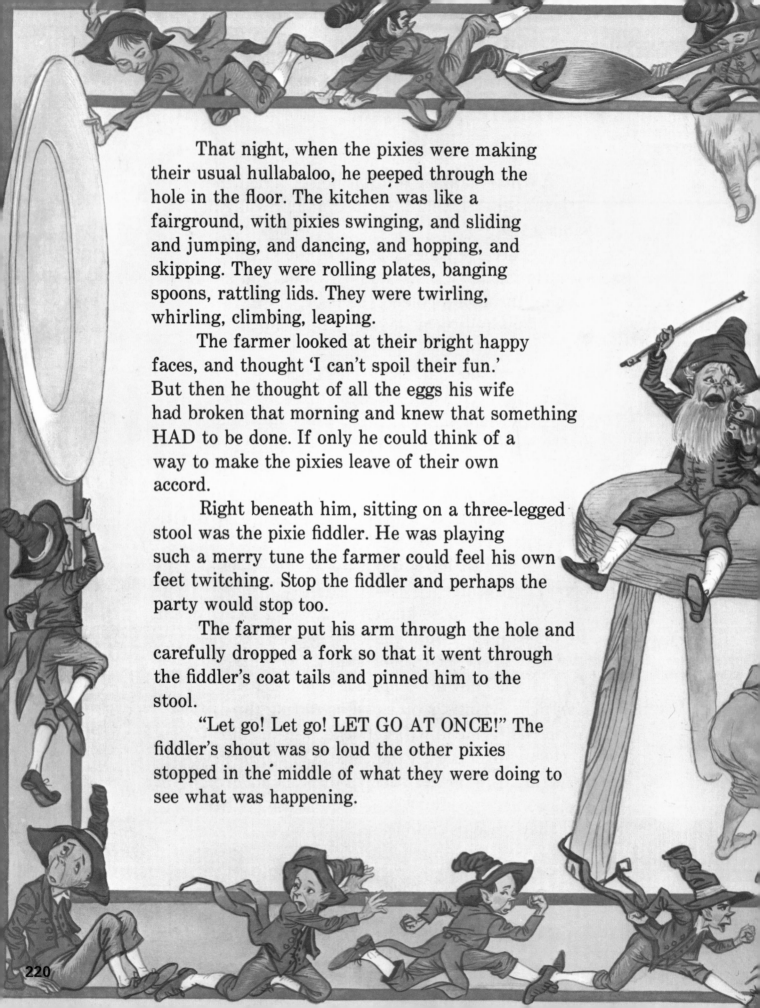

That night, when the pixies were making
their usual hullabaloo, he peeped through the
hole in the floor. The kitchen was like a
fairground, with pixies swinging, and sliding
and jumping, and dancing, and hopping, and
skipping. They were rolling plates, banging
spoons, rattling lids. They were twirling,
whirling, climbing, leaping.

The farmer looked at their bright happy
faces, and thought 'I can't spoil their fun.'
But then he thought of all the eggs his wife
had broken that morning and knew that something
HAD to be done. If only he could think of a
way to make the pixies leave of their own
accord.

Right beneath him, sitting on a three-legged
stool was the pixie fiddler. He was playing
such a merry tune the farmer could feel his own
feet twitching. Stop the fiddler and perhaps the
party would stop too.

The farmer put his arm through the hole and
carefully dropped a fork so that it went through
the fiddler's coat tails and pinned him to the
stool.

"Let go! Let go! LET GO AT ONCE!" The
fiddler's shout was so loud the other pixies
stopped in the middle of what they were doing to
see what was happening.

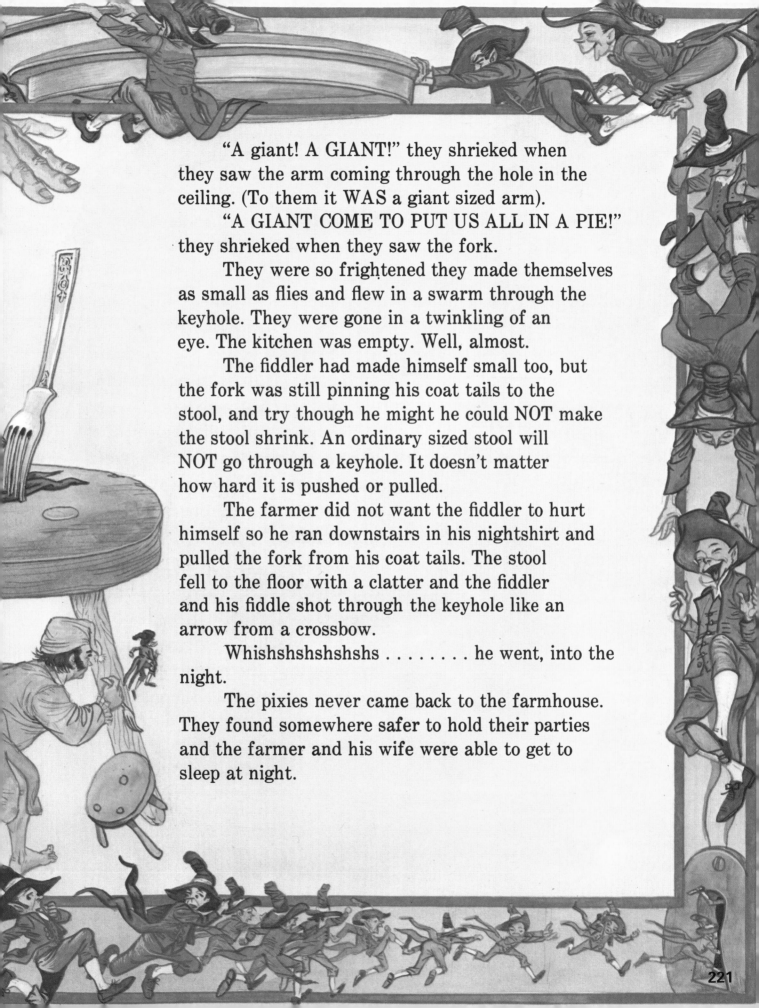

"A giant! A GIANT!" they shrieked when they saw the arm coming through the hole in the ceiling. (To them it WAS a giant sized arm).

"A GIANT COME TO PUT US ALL IN A PIE!" they shrieked when they saw the fork.

They were so frightened they made themselves as small as flies and flew in a swarm through the keyhole. They were gone in a twinkling of an eye. The kitchen was empty. Well, almost.

The fiddler had made himself small too, but the fork was still pinning his coat tails to the stool, and try though he might he could NOT make the stool shrink. An ordinary sized stool will NOT go through a keyhole. It doesn't matter how hard it is pushed or pulled.

The farmer did not want the fiddler to hurt himself so he ran downstairs in his nightshirt and pulled the fork from his coat tails. The stool fell to the floor with a clatter and the fiddler and his fiddle shot through the keyhole like an arrow from a crossbow.

Whishshshshshshs . . . . he went, into the night.

The pixies never came back to the farmhouse. They found somewhere safer to hold their parties and the farmer and his wife were able to get to sleep at night.

A PIG CALLED FANCY

Fancy, the blue pig, opened one eye and peered down through the branches of the big green tree in which he lived. He rustled his wings a little in his cosy nest and then shivered, partly because it was still early in the morning and a little cold, and partly from excitement. Today was the day when he was going on his adventure.

For a long time now, almost since he could remember anything, Fancy had been trying to find out why he was blue and had wings. All the other pigs he knew were pink and lived on the ground. Everyone who met him said "Fancy, a blue pig," until in the end, that was all anyone called him. Fancy didn't know whether he had ever had another name.

He uncurled himself a little further and peered over the edge of his snug home. It was a very long way up in the tree, but that was one of the best things about it, he thought. No one laughed at him up there. The only creatures he talked to were the birds. They took it for granted that anything that lived in a tree could fly. They thought there wasn't anything different at all about Fancy.

The fat little pig clambered out of his nest and unfolded his wings. They were not feathery like a bird's, they were rather silky and very thin, so that when Fancy flew, the sun shone through them and made them sparkle with all the colours of the rainbow. Even though the other pigs laughed at Fancy, he was very proud of his wings.

Avoiding the branches of his tree and the other tall trees nearby, Fancy glided down to earth. He landed with only a little bump.

He was much better at it than he used to be. When he first began to fly, he couldn't manage to land properly at all. He came down with a terrific crash, which left him quite bruised and breathless. Sometimes, he forgot to fold his wings in time, so that he kept bouncing up and down instead of staying on the ground. But now, he was really good. He zoomed in for a superb landing and started looking for breakfast. He snuffled around on the carpet of leaves, looking for nuts and berries. He knew it was very important to eat well before he left on his adventure. After all, who knew where he would be when it came to his next mealtime.

He had a large breakfast and set off. He went North. A long time ago, when Fancy was very small indeed, a visitor had arrived in the forest. He was not like anything anyone had ever seen. He was, everyone supposed, a Cat, but his fur had been bright green. His eyes were gold and glittered when he spoke. The other animals were a little afraid of him, but Fancy had liked him and asked, at once, if the Cat could help him solve his problem.

The golden eyes had glittered, the fur had gleamed greenly in the sunshine and Cat had said, "Go North, that is where your answer lies." Fancy wasn't too good at directions, as he was very young, but he remembered what Cat said. When he was old enough, he had decided that North was where he would go.

He tramped through the forest, deciding to fly when the trees had thinned out a little. The sun could barely reach through the thick forest. Fancy had to keep moving in order to stay warm. The animals he met all seemed busy and not very friendly. There was a snake which hung down from a branch on a tree and gazed at him without speaking. Fancy hurried past – he didn't care for the way the snake was looking at him. Perhaps snakes ate pigs, even blue ones with wings.

A bird with golden red feathers fluttered by. He looked more friendly and so Fancy said, "Excuse me, but am I going North?"

The bird stopped for a moment and gazed at Fancy. "North? Indeed! Why yes, that's the place for you." Then he hurried on. Fancy had begun to feel a little more cheerful when there was a thundering noise behind him. In his fright, he flapped his wings and flew up to the nearest branch where he huddled, very still.

A beautiful white horse thundered through the forest. Fancy looked down as it slowed to a canter beneath his tree. It wasn't a proper horse at all, he thought, for he could see that it had a horn on its forehead. It was . . . it really was a Unicorn. Fancy had heard about Unicorns but he had never thought he would see one. The Unicorn slowed to a walk and it looked up into the tree.

"What are you doing on that branch, little blue pig?" it breathed at Fancy, rather than spoke. Fancy was so scared he nearly fell off his branch. Plucking up all his courage he spoke to the huge animal.

"Where I live all the pigs are pink and they laugh at me. I like to fly and I am proud of my wings, but I want to know why I am different. The Cat that came to our forest said I must go North and that is what I am trying to do."

225

"Come with me, little pig – I too, travel North. You may ride on my back if you think you can stay there," said the Unicorn.

"Oh yes, please," squeaked Fancy. Never in his life had he dreamed of such adventure. To ride on a Unicorn's back. Together they sped through the forest. Fancy had to spread his wings a little now and then to keep his balance, but he managed very well.

Before Fancy knew what had happened, the forest had come to an end. At last he knew why everyone had told him to go North. Before him lay a valley – the sun shone and the grass was green. In the distance a river sparkled and gleamed, small green-furred cats played on the ground and the air was full, just full of blue pigs, with wings of silk which rustled and shone in the light.

Without a backward glance Fancy took off from the Unicorn's back. He was home at last!

King Ferdi And His Dragon

King Ferdi was a kind and happy man. But he hadn't been very happy for some time. He was worried—worried about his pet dragon.

Her name was Dragonia. She was a gentle dragon and full of fun until she went off her food and became droopy. She drooped all over the place and could hardly lift her tail to wag a welcome to her master.

"What's the matter, Dragonia?" he said, rubbing a little soft spot behind her ear. "Tell Ferdi! . . . Why are you so poorly?" Dragonia put her head on his knee, rolled her eyes and gave a big sigh.

The king ordered special meals to be cooked for her. They were served on golden dishes, but Dragonia gave them one sniff and turned away. She was getting thinner every day. King Ferdi was at his wit's end!

He sent for clever doctors. They were afraid to come near her.

"She won't eat you!" roared the king. But they weren't so sure and backed away. He sent for the zoo keepers, but they said: "We have no idea what is wrong, Your Majesty. You see, we don't keep dragons."

He sent for chemists to mix medicine. She shut her jaws—tight!

"What can I do!" wailed the king. "Take her for a walk," suggested the queen. "You keep her indoors too much." Ferdi looked up. "You really think so?" he asked. "Of course!" declared his wife. "Get on your horse and lead her along. It will do you both good." The king in his best hat, and Dragonia in jewelled collar, left the palace.

People poked their heads out of windows. "Fancy! There's the king with his dragon!" They called the children in. "Here comes a dragon!"

Ferdi rode on and out of town. He saw circus tents and led Dragonia towards them. "Get that thing out of here!" a man shouted. "We don't need more animals—can hardly feed what we have!" The king said he was sorry. "My pet won't eat. What do you give your animals?"

"Raw meat for the lions. Hay for horses and elephants. Fish for the seals," answered the man. "Fish!" repeated the king. "Would you sell me some fish?" The man said he could have one to try. "Then you must go," he added. "I can't risk any illness spreading from your poor creature." The king agreed—too upset to be angry. Fish was brought but Dragonia wouldn't touch it. "Could I have a handful of hay?" asked Ferdi. Hay was brought but again Dragonia refused. "Raw meat, now I suppose?" said the circus man rudely. "Yes, please!" said Ferdi politely. But it was useless.

Dragonia wouldn't touch it. The king paid the man and left. When they came to a green shady bank Ferdi stopped to rest. Dragonia flopped down. The horse went under the trees. Soon, all three were asleep.

Presently an old woman passed leading her loaded donkey. She had been to market but had sold nothing. A good smell came from the bundles; Dragonia's nose twitched even as she slept.

Suddenly, the dragon awoke, sniffing the air. Then she was up and following the smell. Hearing shuffling steps, the old woman turned.

"Why, you poor dear!" she cried. "YOU'RE STARVING!" She pulled carrots from the donkey's load and immediately the dragon took a nibble. "That's right, my dear," said the old woman, "slowly now—you'll have a pain if you gobble." Dragonia ate one carrot, then another—and another. The old woman took more from her sack and still Dragonia went on feeding. "I'd like to meet your master!" declared the old woman. "Someone rich by the look of your collar . . . I'd report him to the king!"

When Ferdi awoke he moaned aloud: "Oh dear! Where's my Dragonia?" He searched around: then looked down the road. There sat his dear dragon—gazing at a little old woman and eating! . . . EATING!! "That's enough my dear," she said. "You come along home with me, now. I'm glad I didn't sell my carrots, after all!"

"So am I, madam!" said the king from behind her. The old woman was amazed. "You should be ashamed! Didn't you know your dragon needed carrots?"

The king explained: "We never see raw carrots at the palace!" She offered him one. "Try that, Your Majesty!" Ferdi scrunched—then smiled. "Delicious! How can I reward you?" She shook her head. "I don't need reward, sir."

"Isn't there anything you'd like?" begged Ferdi. Just then his horse appeared. "Yes," she said. "I'd like to ride your beautiful horse and lead your darling dragon!" He laughed: "And so you shall!"

Helping her up he gave her Dragonia's lead. He led the donkey. They set off together and do you know—they were all eating carrots!

Goldilocks and the Three Bears

Once there were three bears. A father bear, a mother bear and a baby bear.

One morning Mother Bear made the porridge for breakfast as usual. "The porridge is exceedingly hot this morning," said Mother Bear.

"Let us go for a stroll in the wood while it cools," said Father Bear.

There was someone else walking in the wood that morning. A little girl with long golden hair, called Goldilocks. She could smell the beautiful aroma of porridge and she followed it, her nose twitching, until she came to the open window of the Bears' house. When she saw the three bowls of steaming porridge on the table they made her feel so hungry she climbed in through the window without so much as a 'please may I?'

"I think I'll try some of that," she said. She tried the porridge in the large bowl first. It was so hot it burnt her tongue.

"Ouch!" she said, and dropped the spoon.

The porridge in the middle size bowl was far too sweet.

"Ugh!" she said, and dropped that spoon too.

The porridge in the small bowl was just the way she liked it.

"Ooh lovely!" she said, and ate it all up.

When the small bowl was quite, quite empty she walked around the house opening cupboards, and looking at this, and looking at that, and trying everything she could see.

She sat on Father Bear's big chair.

"Oh no . . ." she said, "This is much too hard."

She sat on Mother Bear's middle size chair.

"Oh no . . ." she said, "This is much too soft."

She sat on Baby Bear's chair.

"Ooh lovely!" she said. "This is so comfortable."

But she wriggled and fidgeted about so much that one of the legs snapped in two and she fell to the floor.

She picked herself up and went into the bear's bedroom.

She tried Father Bear's big bed.

"Oh no . . ." she said. "This is much too bumpy."

She tried Mother Bear's middle size bed.

"Oh no . . ." she said, "This is much too squashy."

She tried Baby Bear's small bed.

"Ooh lovely!" she said, "This is so comfortable." And she fell fast asleep with her head on Baby Bear's pillow.

When the bears got home they could tell at once that someone had been inside their house.

"Who has been eating my porridge?" growled Father Bear.

"Who has been eating my porridge?" growled Mother Bear.

"And who has been eating my porridge, and finished it all up?" squeaked Baby Bear.

"Who has been sitting on my chair?" growled Father Bear.

"Who has been sitting on my chair?" growled Mother Bear.

"And who has been sitting on my chair, and broken it?" squeaked Baby Bear and he burst into tears.

"Who has been lying on my bed?" growled Father Bear.
"Who has been lying on my bed?" growled Mother Bear.
"Someone has been lying on my bed and she is still here," squeaked Baby Bear. "LOOK!"

Goldilocks opened her eyes and sat up. When she saw the three bears staring at her she jumped off the bed and out through the window so quickly the bears were taken by surprise.

The bears didn't bother to chase after her. She looked so frightened they knew she had learned her lesson and would never go uninvited into someone else's house again.

Instead, Mother Bear made some more porridge for Baby Bear. Father Bear mended his chair. And then they all sat down and had breakfast.

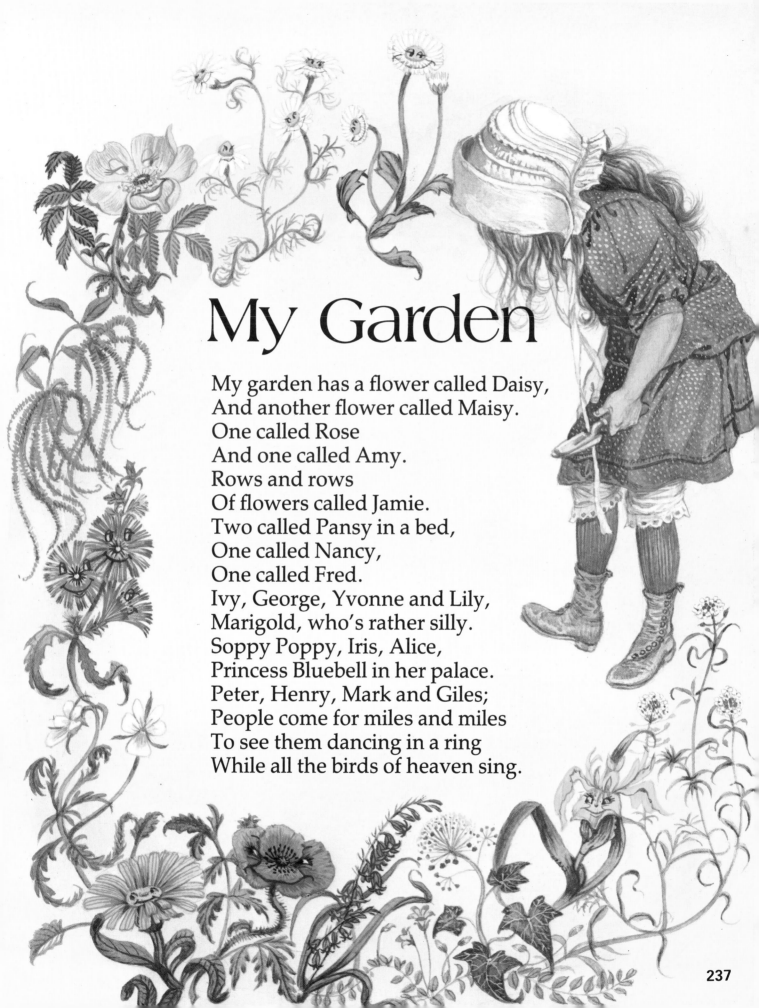

My Garden

My garden has a flower called Daisy,
And another flower called Maisy.
One called Rose
And one called Amy.
Rows and rows
Of flowers called Jamie.
Two called Pansy in a bed,
One called Nancy,
One called Fred.
Ivy, George, Yvonne and Lily,
Marigold, who's rather silly.
Soppy Poppy, Iris, Alice,
Princess Bluebell in her palace.
Peter, Henry, Mark and Giles;
People come for miles and miles
To see them dancing in a ring
While all the birds of heaven sing.